D0742791

JOE R. LANSDALE

This special signed edition is limited to

2000

numbered copies.

This is copy 1873.

Jane Goes NORTH

Jane Goes NORTH

JOE R. LANSDALE

Subterranean Press 2020

First Edition

ISBN
978-1-59606-938-1

Subterranean Press
PO Box 190106
Burton, MI 48519

subterraneanpress.com

Manufactured in the United States of America

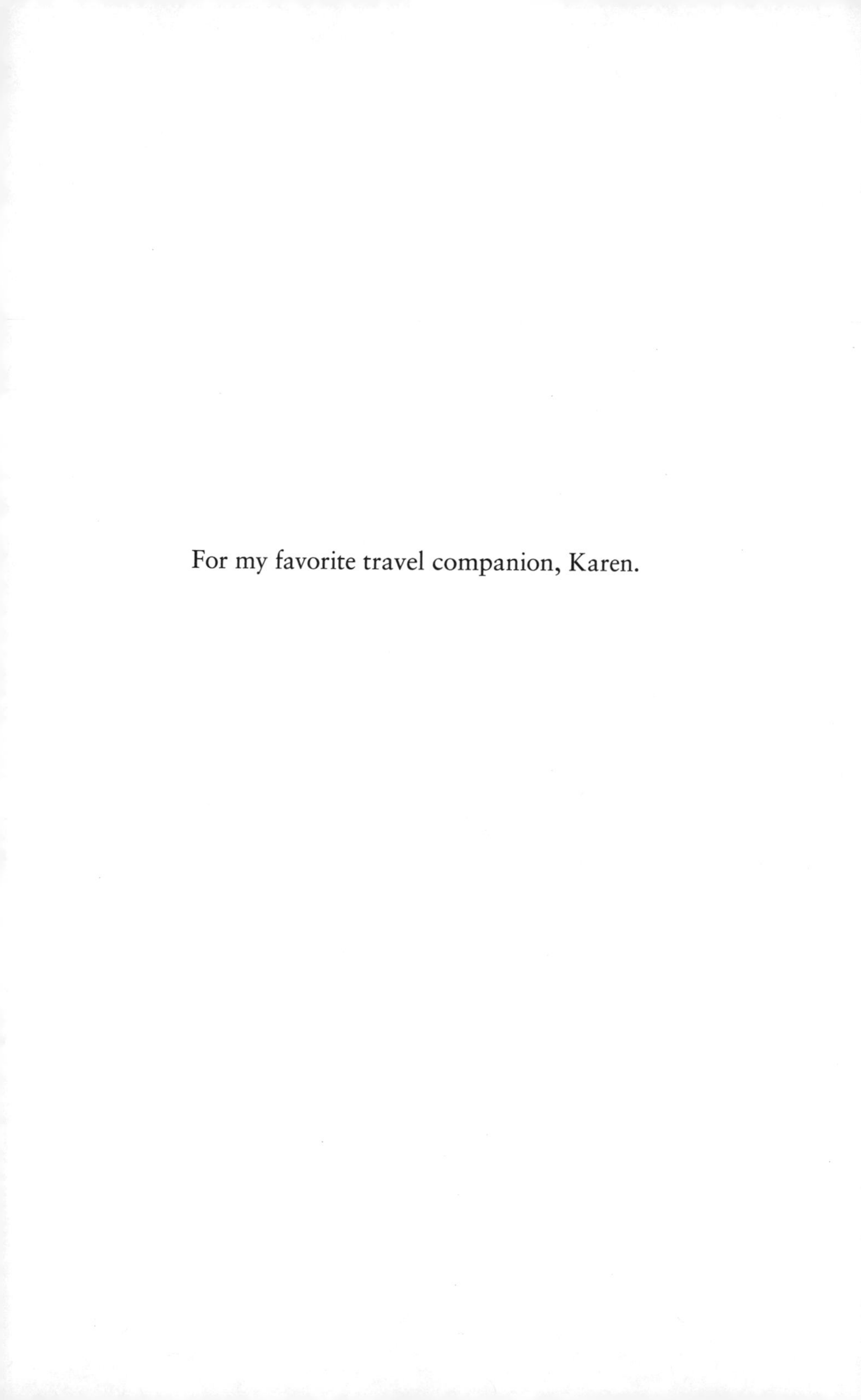

For my favorite travel companion, Karen.

"I have found out that there ain't no surer way to find out whether you like people or hate them than to travel with them."

MARK TWAIN,
TOM SAWYER ABROAD

ONE

JANE got a note in the mail that said her younger sister, Ronnie, was getting married in a place called Ernest City. It was up north, and Jane didn't really want to go. She knew it would be cold up there and a plane flight would be costly and she would have to buy a new suitcase, and on top of it all, she and her sister didn't get along all that well. She was surprised she had been invited, and decided it was meant to be a polite invitation, and no one really expected her to come.

That made her want to go. It had always been that way with her. You tried to talk her out of something, she was damn sure going to do it. This had resulted in two ex-husbands, a failed mortgage, a small scar on her left cheek, and a lot of beauty supplies she hadn't been able to sell. When her mother was alive, she said, "Jane, them supplies you got to pay for yourself if you don't sell them, and you couldn't sell a step stool to a midget."

"I think they like being called Little People," Jane said.

"Well, you couldn't sell one to them neither."

Jane had spited her mother for years in all manner of things to prove her wrong, and just last birthday, turning thirty, she realized she had in fact been proving her right for years. Though she kind of thought she might actually have been able to sell a step stool to someone that was short, on account of they might need it.

She wasn't sure she could go to the wedding anyway, because she was on what might be called a limited budget. Which meant she had been fired at the laundry where she had been working for eight years, and was living off her savings, such as it was. The firing had been unfair. Some rich lady's clothes had been ruined when they got cleaned and pressed, but the way Jane saw it, it was the lady's fault for leaving a package of ketchup from Burger King in a pocket. She couldn't look through every pocket on every pair of pants or dress, or such, and have it all done by Tuesday.

Didn't work like that.

But here she was, wondering how she was going to pay for her trailer and the rent on her lot, and her with a wedding to go to. She started to not be stubborn, just decide to not go and make everyone happy, maybe send a cheap gift from the Dollar General, though in a couple of weeks, the bills she owed would be compounded and the best she might be able to send were a few laundry tips, the most important being "Watch out for ketchup packets in pockets. They can break open and ruin stuff."

What she didn't understand about Ronnie, was why was she getting married anyway. She and her boyfriend, Fred

Clipper, had been living together for five years and already had a two-year-old baby and a basset hound. It seemed funny to her these days that the way it worked was you lived together until you got pregnant, and then you got married. The dog could be optional, wedded or not.

This seemed ass-backwards to Jane, but times were a changing, and in fact, had changed about twenty years ago when she was ten, but she hadn't been paying attention.

She finally decided that if she was going to go, she was going to have to take a bus. Then she thought about the time she had been on a school trip when she was sixteen, and how sick she got riding on a bus. She could still smell the diesel fumes and Marilyn Cover's sack lunch; it had some kind of foul-smelling meat packed against some kind of foul-smelling cheese, between thick, chewy bread with seeds on it. Come to think of it, Marilyn was the kind of girl that might keep ketchup packets in pockets.

Jane thought it might be fun to leave early, take her time, and drive about and see the country, not that she had the money for it, and her car wasn't much of one. It got her back and forth from work when she had a job at the laundry, but driving it way up north didn't seem likely. She might not manage to get far out of town before her junker fell apart, leaving her beside the road with cars blowing by.

Hitchhiking was a thought, but being as she felt she was a comely woman, she might attract unwanted attention, and might even be picked up by a serial killer or a mass murderer, or a Jehovah's Witness, so she checked that off her list.

Then she remembered something. This ride-sharing thing they had down at the college. They tacked things up on a board for people to see, and it was listed on the internet as well. Not being able to work the internet, and not even owning a cell phone or a computer due to financial difficulties, Jane tied her hair back and drove over to the university, and after driving around in the visitor parking section waiting for someone to leave so she could park, she finally saw a small car back out. It was driven by a blonde girl who drove like she thought she couldn't be killed. She backed out quick and without looking nearly ran over Jane's hunk of junk, and then drove off, maybe never knowing she had nearly clipped a car behind her.

Jane had an urge to follow her, and when she stopped somewhere, give her a few driving guidelines, but she decided she didn't have enough gas for unnecessary running around, and any strain on her old car might be too much, like having sex with an eighty-year-old husband without having seen the will.

Jane parked and walked over to the student union building. She found the board with the rides pinned to it. There were only three little cards requesting shared rides, and the rest of the board was filled with ads for upcoming events. As for the rides, all three wanted to ride in someone else's car, which considering this was what Jane wanted to do, didn't help much.

Back home Jane thought about it, and finally decided she was damn sure going to go to the wedding and she was going to chance it in her car. She thought if she left in the cool of the night, the car might be less inclined to heat up. It was an old car and the radiator loved to get hot and spill and steam water out of it, but that was partly because it was an

East Texas summer and so damn hot during the day a lizard needed a straw hat. But at night it would be somewhat cooler, and she could stop and rest through the day some place. She didn't really have money for many nights at a motel, but she might pull into truck stops and sleep in her car. Some folks said a Save-Mart parking lot, since the stores were open twenty-four hours, was a great place to park your car and sleep. She thought too, as she got farther north, the weather would be cooler and less stress on her radiator.

It was the only idea she could come up with. She gave it a day to think about, didn't change her mind when morning came, so she packed up and put some canned beans in a box, and put those in the back seat of the car, along with her day to day needs: makeup, clothes, shoes and such, a sack lunch, as well as her one nice little black dress to wear to the wedding. She felt it would be fine, since the wedding was to be casual. It wasn't like she had been asked to be a bridesmaid, or to even serve punch.

Her other sisters would be there. They were all right. Better than Ronnie, her entitled, snotty, younger sister. The other two had both married into money and lived not far from the youngest, so it wasn't the same burden for them to go, and they were only part time assholes, though they were jealous of her, and always had been. Jane thought it was because she was the pretty sister, but then it often occurred to her that maybe they just didn't like her, and perhaps she wasn't likeable. It was a possibility.

Jane had driven about five miles out of town when the car started to act up. She pulled over beside the road and opened the hood like she knew what she was doing. She watched the radiator cough white smoke into the air for a while, then closed the hood. She had learned nothing except her car wasn't running and might possibly be on fire.

A few minutes later a man who was close to ninety years old if he was a minute, pulled over in a pickup truck and got out. He managed himself over to her car with a determination fitting a Spartan warrior; it took him so long to get there, Jane thought he might die before he arrived, but he finally showed up with sweaty armpits and a determined look.

"You got a problem?" he asked.

This seemed obvious, but Jane said, "I do. Do you know anything about cars?"

"I couldn't fix a wheelbarrow with new parts," he said.

"Oh."

"What I can do is give you a ride somewhere."

"Back to town," she said.

On the way back, she learned the old man was named Luther and had a prostate problem but it had never kept him from getting it up when he needed to, though he made it abundantly clear he wasn't referring to her as a possible subject to demonstrate his ability, just passing the time of day with his ailment. But when he dropped her off at the mechanic's he gave her his phone number on a fast food sack and wrote next to it, "In case you get bored."

The mechanic drove her out to her car in his wrecker and looked it over. He was a long, greasy shirted man with a frayed cap that seemed to perch on his head more than fit on it. He spat a lot of tobacco while he looked under the hood, some of which found its way onto the engine, causing it to steam a little. He also managed to spit on Jane's shoe.

"It's real hot," he said.

"I noted that," she said, shaking the tobacco from her shoe with a vigorous wiggle of her foot.

He saw her do that, but didn't comment.

"I mean the car's hot, not the weather," he said.

"Got that too."

"It's got a busted radiator."

"How do you fix it?"

"With a new radiator."

"Can it be patched?"

"Only if you plan to back it in and out of your driveway now and again. It goes any kind of distance, or you drive it over thirty miles an hour for long, it's going to blow."

"How much is a new radiator?"

He told her, and then he told her how much the cost of the installation would be.

Jane said, "How much just to haul it back to my house?"

JANE sat in the kitchen of her mobile home, which was about the size of a cat box, and drank a cup of instant coffee and ate the lunch she had packed for the trip. She sat there and thought her sister might have to do without her, but the idea of that bothered her, because that would give Ronnie ammunition to think things weren't good with her financially, which they weren't. But she didn't want that bitch to know it. She didn't want any of her sisters to know, as her failure in life was all they wished for, Ronnie wishing the hardest.

Jane determined once again, as she did several times a day, that all the sisters had a beef with her because she was the good looking one, though sometimes her love for pizza broadened her ass. Course, lately, she couldn't afford pizza, and had been living mostly off instant oatmeal and rice cakes and tunafish sandwiches, and the occasional banana. Did that, your ass stayed small but your stomach stayed hungry.

Jane decided to walk down to the university and look in on the pin-up board again, see if anyone else had added a note since yesterday. It seemed unlikely, but she was short on ideas.

There was a blackened banana on top of the refrigerator in a bowl, and she took that with her as she walked to the university, eating it with one hand while she held her purse against her side with the other to keep it from swinging on the strap.

It was certainly a less pleasant trip on foot than it was by car, but at least she didn't have to worry about a parking place, or some blonde kamikaze running over her in the parking lot.

When she got to the university, she was sticky-hot, and it was nice to go inside where the information board and the air-conditioning were.

The board had a few notes on it, but only one new one for a ride share. The other notes were trying to sell things. Jane called the number on the new ride share, and after speaking to a voice that sounded as if the speaker chain-smoked cigarettes and drank ground glass with whisky, she discovered the woman, Henrietta, lived about three blocks away on Mercy Street.

"I'm up there between two brick houses," Henrietta said. "Mine's the one made of wood."

Now, if there had been a straw house on the street, the entire Three Little Pigs fable would be completed, provided Jane was willing to play the wolf.

She thought the name of the street, Mercy, was a good omen, so she walked over there. When she arrived at the door of the number she had been given, she paused and took a handkerchief from her purse and wiped the sweat from her face. After she put the hankie away, she knocked on the door, and within instants a woman tall enough to play on a basketball team answered. She had stringy dark hair that might have been washed in the Great Flood, and was wearing a colorful, knee-length house dress with all the fine lines and artistry of a circus tent, and fuzzy blue house shoes. The dress showed her lower legs to be muscular and bruised, and though Jane tried not to concentrate on it, she saw that the woman had one dead eye that wandered as if drunk or drugged. The other was as steel-gray as a battleship and was focused on her like a laser.

"Excuse me," Jane said. "Are you—"

"Henrietta," said the woman, "but everyone calls me Henry. Except my mother. She calls me Henrietta. Or did."

"That makes sense," Jane said. "I saw your ad. I'm Jane Gardner and I live over on Swamp Road, but there isn't any swamp there. I live right across from the big Baptist church, or what used to be one and is now a kind of dollar store."

Henry became rigid as stone. "The one where the preacher and his organist were caught fucking in a SUV in the rear parking lot?"

Jane's cheeks flushed red. "That's the one."

"That bastard and that goddamn skank."

Henry's comment embarrassed Jane a little, because she had been the fuckee, though she wasn't an organist, just a church goer. She never corrected the common but odd misconception that it was an organist, as therefore the trail didn't lead as directly to her. It had turned out the church didn't have an organist, but the rumor persisted. The preacher, one Reverend Seymore Wagoner, who she had met at a beer joint on the Southside of town, had decamped the next day, and had moved off to Maybank, or someplace like that. Rumor was he was selling used cars or insurance, and sometimes the rumor had him as a member of a motorcycle gang made up of angry Christians, which seemed to be the most common kind these days. Angry Muslims. Angry Christians. Cranky Buddhist—she knew one, a lady that worked at the dollar store. Religion seemed to bring out the worst in folks.

Jane wondered what the odds were of the fuckee event being mentioned first crack out of the box when meeting a stranger. It made her nervous, even if she was certain Henry didn't know she was the one who had diddled the preacher. The preacher may not have even known she was the one he had diddled. He was shit-blind drunk, and not with the Holy Ghost. He could have been handed a doughnut to screw, and he would have named it Shirley, and he was maybe one beer short of death by alcohol.

She had been lonely and the preacher dressed well enough, except for a pair of white loafers that looked to have time traveled from the seventies. Jane had about as much church in her as a squirrel, but she had liked the way his jib was set, so to speak—a comment her father used to make which she thought might have relevance—and one thing led to another. She and he left the bar in his SUV, her driving because she was the less drunk of the two. In the parking lot they switched to the back seat and came together quickly, so to speak, and though the idea of it being a church parking lot embarrassed her a little, it was not as much as the fact that the lot had once been home to a Whataburger, and now it had been razed again and was a dollar store.

Fortunately they didn't do a lot of talking, so life stories and general information were not exchanged. Therefore, she hadn't told the preacher where she lived, or that she had first seen him across the street in the doorway of the church smiling and shaking hands with his flock as they exited his Sunday sermon. He had no idea she knew he was a preacher, and it seemed that night neither did he.

A cop car came flashing its lights while they were in the act, and Jane was mercifully not revealed as the Reverend's sex partner, mostly because she ran butt-ass naked clutching her clothes down into the creek behind the church. From there, she finally got dressed and worked her way around and to her house without being identified, unless some wildlife was talking.

The police report in the weekly newspaper said the naked lady who ran away "was swift." Fucking a preacher wasn't a crime, but it certainly could have been embarrassing in a public way.

Jane was thinking on all of this when Henry spoke again.

"Come in, sit down. Tell me about yourself."

Jane went in, passed a weight bench and weights, and sat down at the kitchen table with Henry. There were some cookies on a plate. They looked like small cow chips, only drier. The air inside was stale and smelled unpleasant.

"Want some coffee?" Henry said.

"That would be nice."

"Anything in it?"

"Black is fine."

Henry made coffee with one of those machines with the little containers you put in per cup, and Jane found herself envious. She always had instant and had to heat the water in a pan on the stove. Then she noted that the little capsules Henry used already had holes in them. She was running them through a second time, but Jane smiled and pretended not to notice. The coffee was barely dark, and tasted like hot water strained through a dead cat's ass.

In fact, now that she looked about the kitchen, the house for that matter, seemed shabbier than her own, as if it had once housed a large family and pets that had moved off suddenly and left Henry alone with a full cat box and no fresh coffee.

Jane took one of the cookies, which she realized were home baked, and felt the heft of it in her hand. She dipped it into her coffee, but eating the cookie was still a work out. Two more dips proved fruitless. It was like trying to dissolve a chunk of obsidian. She placed it next to her coffee cup, as if she had intention to pursue it in the near future.

Henry examined her with her one good eye. The other was on a walkabout. Jane hated the way she felt about Henry's eye. It made her feel like a bad person, but the eye was making her nervous. She thought it might be a good idea for Henry to get a patch to wear over it to keep it from being a distraction. It was hard to concentrate when the eye had a mind of its own. She figured she said something about it, suggested a patch, it would just be rude, and maybe she was the one in the wrong for noticing the eye, but, if you noticed a limp, did that mean you hated cripples? She thought not.

She artfully remained silent on the matter. Jane moved her gaze a little so she could see out a window that looked right into the carport, which had obviously been added on. She could see Henry's car in there, and it was banged up and scraped and the windshield was cracked. She didn't know how the other side looked, but that side went with the dead eye, and Jane began to think a long trip with a bad-eye driver might not be the best choice.

"It'll be a fun trip," Henry said, pulling Jane's attention back to her.

"Is that your car?" Jane said, knowing the answer, but unable not to ask.

"It is. Little roughed up. It got scraped on some other cars."

"They run into you?"

"No, I sort of scraped them parallel parking."

"Oh."

"Police said I shouldn't be drinking while driving, but I had only had a couple of beers. And a shot or two. I forget exactly. But I wasn't drunk. I've always had trouble with curbs and such. I don't have a license anymore, actually."

"I suppose I would drive?"

This seemed to cause dark waters to rise in Henry.

"I don't let other people drive my car. You understand? I like to be in control."

"I see. Are both sides of the car banged up?"

"You're asking if I have trouble because of my eye, aren't you?"

"Well..."

"A little. Is that going to be a problem? Are you one of those that judge people by their disabilities?"

"I don't know it's a judgment, but I suppose it's a consideration," Jane said.

"A consideration?"

Henry slowly put the cup of coffee she was sipping on the coaster on the table, doing so in the tedious manner a bomb tech might use when disarming something explosive. Jane noticed the bulge of muscle in her forearm and knew immediately who lifted the weights in the living room, and it wasn't an ex-husband or boyfriend.

"You're one of them kind, aren't you?"

"No," Jane said. "I don't think so. But, thinking about safety, certain factors ought to be considered."

"Like what?"

"You don't have a license."

"That, huh?"

"Kind of a big deal."

"I can drive with a license or without one."

"But you're not supposed to."

"Have you ever broken the law?"

"I don't think so, though I once ran a red light by accident," Jane said, and tried not to let Henry know she was measuring the distance to the front door.

"I'm thinking you're not a nice person, and I don't think I want to go anywhere with you."

"I'm feeling the same. I'd rather go up north on a pogo stick than ride with you. With your eye, I bet you can't do nothing but make messy left turns in a demolition derby."

Jane hated she had said it the moment it came out of her mouth, but it was done and she had to live with it.

"I think you're a mean bitch," Henry said.

"And I'm thinking you ought to get an eye patch and about ten years of psychiatry. And while you're at it, you might want to buy some fresh coffee and some cookies that aren't so hard you could build a fence with them, or for that matter, a goddamn house, though you'd have to bake a lot of them."

Henry stood up quickly, and from the look in her one eye, Jane knew she might be in trouble. She jumped up and made a dash for the door. She was almost there when she felt a sharp pain in the back of her head and heard something clatter to the floor and spin out in front of her. It was one of the cookies. Jane was surprised at Henry's aim, considering she had so much trouble parking her car.

Jane opened the door and leaped down the steps and ran toward the road.

Another cookie whizzed by her ear with deadly intent and smacked onto the sidewalk. Those weights had certainly given Henry the throwing arm of a professional baseball player.

Behind her she heard Henry yell out, "Least I got a car, and some manners, you ole bitch."

Jane turned and looked back. Henry was standing on her front porch, armed with the plate of cookies.

"You come back up in here I'll knock you out."

"You got the cookies for it," Jane said.

"A rock would throw better," Henry said. "I had one of those, I could hit you all the way down the road there."

"I don't think so," Jane said. "That's just wishful thinking."

"Is it?" Henry said, and another cookie flew.

It was a damn solid throw, and just missed her.

"I tell you, I had a rock, I could clock you," Henry said.

Henry said something else, but by that point it was only a noise, as Jane was walking away quickly.

From time to time, Jane looked back to see if Henry might be following her with the plate of cookies, or had found a rock or two, but she didn't see her.

By the time she walked back to her house, it was well past noon, and she was sweaty and could smell herself. Where she had been hit in the back of the head was throbbing. That was one firm cookie. Henry had probably forgotten to put eggs in the mix, or had substituted Gorilla Glue.

Jane pulled a jug of milk from the refrigerator, poured herself a glass, and discovered that it had gone sour. She poured the milk in the glass and the contents of the jug down the sink.

The trip up north was beginning to look unlikely.

TWO

AFTER a shower, Jane felt better and the cookie injury had begun to subside, thanks to a couple of Tylenols and running hot water over the bump on her head. She put on a loose cotton dress and turned on the TV, and put it on one of the shopping channels. She had never bought a thing from the shopping channel, but she found it soothed her, looking at things she might like to have if she had money to spare or someone wanted to give her something.

She made a cup of instant coffee, which after Henry's coffee, seemed outstanding. Now she was back at square one, and it looked to her that she was not about to move off of it.

But the more she sat and thought about it, the more she was bothered by not going. She wanted to show them she could and would show up, and she would have a gift too, something beyond just her best wishes. She tried to think of an appropriate gift, but all she could come up with was an egg timer, because she saw it on the shopping channel, but who the hell really needed an egg timer? It was like underwear and a beret for a dog. Unnecessary.

But there was still the problem of gift money, and even more important, how to make the trip. She decided she had a day or two to think about a solution, but no more than that.

The shopping channel had ceased to amuse her. She found a movie about a truck driver who had been done wrong and was going to get even by running over people with his truck; at least, she thought that was what it was about. Her mind kept drifting. But she was certain a lot of people got ran over.

That night, as she got ready for bed, she was still without any kind of solution, and in the night, she dreamed of seeing Henry on the road in her battered car, and the car had a patch over one of its headlights, and it was zooming down the road, lit up by impossibly bright moonlight.

Henry was driving with her knees and had a coffee cup in one hand and one of those rock-like cookies in the other. She was jetting along a two-lane blacktop, and then there were lights. The lights were coming out of the woods, and it was a big ole truck pulling a long, silver trailer, and now Jane could see she was driving the truck, sitting behind the wheel with both hands clutching it, and she was leaning forward, grinning from ear to ear, and then she drove right into Henry, knocked that banged-up clunker across the road, throwing Henry clear of the car and out into a field of red flowers.

Henry stood up from her fall, still holding the cup of coffee in one hand and the cookie in the other. As Jane bore down on her in the truck, Henry tossed the cookie with a savage outlet of breath, and the cookie cracked the truck's windshield with a bullet-like sound. And then Jane lost control of the truck and the trailer jackknifed and the truck turned over, and she found herself tumbling down a hill, being bounced around inside the truck cab like a ball bearing in a paint can.

Jane woke up on the floor wrapped in her sheets as if she were inside a cocoon.

"Damn," she said.

AFTER a cup of coffee, she considered a few ideas to make enough money to travel north. She thought she might earn enough to get her car fixed if she walked down to the corner of 69 and the loop, and stood out there with a cardboard sign that said, "I have lost my home and car and am looking for enough money to buy room and board. I might like to get a little dog to go with it."

She had seen a lot of similar signs and a lot of men and women, some with dogs, at that corner, and she had even seen people stop there and give money to them, especially anyone with a dog. She didn't have a dog, but a hopeful sign about one might be encouraging enough for a delayed driver at the light to let go of some money.

Once, she had given a dollar to a poor looking man with an artificial leg and a pit bull that slept on a large grungy white towel during the transaction. For all she could tell, it might have died in its sleep, but the next day when she went by the corner, the pit bull was in the short grass near the overpass taking a dump and the man with the sign was still there looking pathetic and lonesome. She didn't give him a dollar a second time. She had heard that some of those people made a whole lot of money and drove very fine cars. She had doubts about that. Most of them looked as if they were about to have a stroke or die of gas fumes from passing cars, but the notion there might be a nation of highly successful grifters with mansions and limousines to go home to at night allowed her to keep a tight grip on her dollar.

Still, that whole begging thing might be a way to add enough to her coffers to get done what she needed to get done. She could show a little leg if she had to, wear something nice. Though, come to think of it, that might throw off her whole plan. If she looked too nice, or sexy, she might be thought to be a prostitute trying to move upscale, or a music teacher on her way down, meaning there might still be money in her bank account, and her need would be far less than a fellow with a bum leg and a sleepy pit bull. A prostitute on her way up might fare better than a descending teacher, but maybe the best bet was to wear old pants and a T-shirt with some kind of slogan on it. Something tasteful.

She had one with a teddy bear and the words, GIVE ME A HUG, I WANT IT stenciled on it.

Of course, she figured by the time anyone quit looking at the cute teddy bear, and was about to read the words on the T-shirt, the light would have changed, so maybe that wasn't a good choice. She needed them focused on her cardboard beg sign.

She decided maybe she ought to wear a light, short sleeve shirt that could help her withstand the heat, slightly worn jeans, and loose shoes and that would make her look more neutral. Without makeup and with her hair tied back, a Huck Finn straw hat on her head, she felt she could get away with looking sad, like her husband had left her and she had made a bad investment in pork belly futures. It wasn't a good plan, but it was a plan, and she was determined to make the trip to her sister's wedding. The actuality of the plan began to fade as she realized how stupid it was. Besides, she might have to fight the fellow already there, along with his pit bull. That's when she heard a horn honking and went to a living room window, pulled back the curtain and looked out.

Setting in her drive was Henry's battered wreck, and Henry was behind the wheel. Henry had run over one of the next-door neighbor's rose bushes and had turned Jane's mail box around as if it was on a swivel. She barely missed Jane's wreck which was parked in the driveway.

Henry had a popsicle stick hanging from her lips as she got out of the car. Unlike the dream, she didn't have coffee or cookies and the car didn't have an eye patch over one headlight.

THREE

"AH, hell," Jane said.

Jane eased the front door open a crack, yelled out at Henry as she came up the drive. "You aren't going to try and hit me with another cookie, are you?"

"I'm out of cookies," Henry said.

"I bet it isn't because someone ate them."

A dark cloud crawled across Henry's face, but it was blown aside instantly, and a smile that would have shamed a velociraptor took its place. "I'd like to talk to you, see if we can straighten things out."

"You haven't got any weapons on you, do you?"

"A paring knife, but I always carry that."

"I don't care if you just carry it from time to time, put it down on the walk there."

Henry was wearing a clunky dress that was constructed of voluminous pleats of blue and white cloth. It was hitched up in places that left folds. It seemed to be designed for massive growth or shrinkage of its owner. From inside one of the dress folds, Henry produced the paring knife, and placed it on the concrete walk.

"I didn't have to do that," Henry said. "I could have just come in on you, kicked that door off its hinges, and beat your ass with one of your own chairs."

"Maybe we ought to talk through the door."

"I need to go north, bad, and you want to go as well. I think we got off on a bad foot. I'm sensitive about my driving and the confiscation of my license."

"That's what happens when you run over every damn thing in sight."

"I actually didn't see what I ran over."

"My mailbox for one, and my next-door neighbor's rose bush."

Henry looked back. "That old thing? She calls that a rose bush?"

"She'll call it dead now."

"Come on, girl. Why don't you invite me in?"

"The paring knife stays where it is."

"NOW, you got to get up north, and so do I, and I haven't got enough money to go, and neither do you or you wouldn't be trying to bum a ride with me, but if we go on ahead and do as we planned, put our money together and take the trip together, we can get there."

Jane listened to Henry, as they sat in the living room without cookies or coffee. Henry had discarded her popsicle stick by placing it on a coaster on the coffee table. The gooey residue on the stick caused it to stick there, and Jane tried to ignore it.

Jane cleared her throat. "Listen now, I don't want you to go all hissy fit on me, but that license thing. That matters."

"Well, I don't drive good as I once did. Things on one side aren't visible, least not unless I hold my head like this, and when I do, then I can't see the other side, and way my bad eye is, well, you got to move your head a lot to see good when driving. Eye's not dead by the way, just deep sleeping. That's why I need to go up north, to Boston. They got a doctor there can fix it, and she does it for people without money, and that's me. Supposed to be able to see out of it better, if not perfect, and she can keep it from roaming and make the color come back in it."

This sounded doubtful and overly rehearsed to Jane, but she did want to go to that wedding.

"You still didn't say about the driving situation."

"I'm saying you can drive my car, and I'll just be a passenger. You'll be my chauffeur. That's what we can tell people."

"You barely got a car, who's going to believe you have a chauffeur for that ole wreck?"

A stiff posture invaded Henry's body, and for a moment she looked as if she might leap from her chair, over the coffee table, and onto Jane.

Jane prepared to give her life dearly, but then Henry seemed to lose whatever demon had stiffened her, and she sat back loosely in the chair and sighed.

"I've always been a bit testy," Henry said. "Comes from being called names as a kid. 'Hey, Cyclops. What's up, One

Eye. You're pretty. Pretty ugly and apt to stay that way. How long you been dead? And how'd you manage to dig out of your grave? If you had a dick, you could be a horse, one of the ugly ones.'"

"That's terrible."

"Heard it all my life."

"Kids are the worst."

"Oh, that was my mama."

"Hell," Jane said.

"Hope she went there. She got hit by a car and killed. I was under suspicion, but when they figured out I was drunk and in jail, well, they let me go. Never did find who run over her. Ever did, I'd have to give them a medal of some sort. I hope it was her goddamn pastor, she loved him so much. 'Why he's got Jesus in his pocket,' she used to say. What he had in his pocket was the Lottie Moon offering and the church bake sale funds. The sonofabitch ran off to Maybank or some such when they found him riding a slut in the parking lot."

Jane felt herself redden again, but even in the same moment, a wave of sympathy for Henry swept over her, as well as a similar wave of fear and caution. Henry seemed like the sort that at the drop of a hat could go off her nut. The kind of person that could shit a brick and call it Tuesday and make you agree. Jane had brief visions of being found dead in a ditch with her purse stolen and her pockets turned inside out, and a hard cookie imbedded in the back of her head.

But the siren call of the wedding sang out to her.

"If I can drive, be your chauffer, as you call it, then we can make this work."

"When's your wedding?"

Jane told her.

"That means we got time see the sights a little, we choose to. And I say we should. I'll be by to get you late morning, say ten, ten-thirty?"

Jane agreed. They shook hands on the deal, and Henry pressed Jane's hand so hard Jane felt her asshole close tight for a moment, and then it was over. The deal was done.

FOUR

NEXT morning, Jane decided to carry more things with her than she had originally planned, and when she started to add more things to her suitcase, the zipper broke and she couldn't close it up.

She bought a good suitcase with roller wheels across the street at the dollar store, where the cranky Buddhist worked. While she was repacking, she thought maybe her black dress wasn't that good a pick for a wedding. Its darkness made it seem more for a funeral than a wedding, but the style of it, way low cut in the front and high hemmed at the bottom, might raise the dead. She concluded she didn't have the perfect dress for a wedding, but if she should want to be a cocktail waitress, she was ready. Jane decided that since she wasn't being asked to be a bridesmaid, a ring girl, or a participant in a greased pig contest, it really didn't matter what kind of dress or what color she wore.

She added a little carryon bag to her possibles, as her father used to call extra gear, and then she went to the bathroom to gather a few toiletries to stick in that bag. An extra toothbrush, deodorant, some first aid stuff, multiple changes of underwear. She was somewhat fanatic about that due to her mother, who had always feared a car wreck would leave one of their family to be discovered in dirty underwear. As her dad said, "Have a bad enough car wreck, I promise you, you'll have dirty underwear."

Finishing up, Jane looked in the mirror, combed her long hair, patted it down on top, then dropped the comb into her purse along with her makeup. The last thing she did was write a note that said if she was missing or found murdered there was a good chance Henry did it. She wrote out Henry's full name and signed the note and put it under a bear shaped sugar bowl on the kitchen table.

She was as ready as she was ever going to be.

FIVE

IN the late afternoon, when Henry came to pick her up, she managed to run over the flower bed again, this time solidly enough to make sure there wouldn't be any chance of survival for the flattened rose bush, which just that morning looked as if it might be trying to rise from the dirt and greet the sun.

The mailbox was spared another clip from Henry's car, and within moments Jane had the house locked up and the suitcase loaded in the trunk of Henry's automobile, next to a flat spare tire and a bag of leaking aluminum cans.

"Figure we can sell the cans somewhere," Henry said. "Might be a dollar, dollar fifty there."

"Okay," Jane said.

Jane had put a few dollars in her purse, but had stuck most of her green backs in her shoes, along with her license, Target and Discover credit cards, both of which were not far from being maxed out, but still contained a few miles of use, and the payments were up to date. It wasn't much, but it was all she had, and it made her seem taller. As the trip progressed, she could imagine herself growing smaller and smaller, like Alice when she drank the drink that made her small. If she used the larger bill denominations, which were in her right shoe, she might even develop a limp.

Neither had a cell phone or a GPS, but Henry produced a map that was marked up so Jane could follow it and be dropped off at the wedding, and then Henry, providing she didn't run over anyone or peel the side of the car off while going through a drive-through, could finish her journey to the eye doctor. That was not marked on the map. As for Jane going home, that hadn't been worked out. Jane was hoping she might be able to manage bus fare for that, but since the price of the trip, gas and food and such, would be costly, she was uncertain, and decided to deal with that situation when she came to it.

As Henry gave Jane the car keys, she said, "Driver's seat belt hangs a little, so you might have to wrestle it a bit. And the car kind of veers to the right. I used to operate farm machinery that responded better."

Jane thought that it was Henry who veered to the right, not the car, but when she backed out and was on the road, she found that indeed, the car wanted to drift right, and it made her need to fight the wheel to stay off the grass and gravel.

Soon, Jane felt she had the hang of it. You had to keep a firm hand on the wheel, as if you were gripping the horns of a bull that you were trying to rodeo to the ground.

They went along not talking for some time, and Jane decided that she might as well try and start and carry a conversation, even if it was about the weather, which was hot, but it was like hauling a concrete block strapped on your head to the top of Mt. Everest. It was a lot of work and wasn't worth it. Henry responded with grunts and yes and no, and all of it sounded reluctant, like a teenager having to listen to a lecture on not driving the car too fast and to make sure water was in the radiator and the tires were checked.

Considering the condition of her car, Jane wished she had paid more attention to just such a discussion from her now dead dad, who had warned her of such consequences and had given her suggestions.

"Looks will only get you so far," he used to say, "and then one day, they won't even get you very far. And remember, a car is like a person. It heats up, and it needs a drink. Keep water in the radiator, and for heaven's sake, check the goddamn air in the tires."

After a few more attempts at conversation, Jane settled into a silence that seemed to suit both herself and Henry. The tires hummed on the concrete, and it was a relaxing sound, like listening to an old-style window fan at night, beating a kind of dreamy rhythm. She had one in her bedroom window as a child. Back then she dreamed of becoming something of consequence, which then was a bride, a housewife and mother. In the dreams, once married, she would have a little white dog that was well trained, and like Lassie, if she were to fall into a well or break a leg in the woods, the dog would go for help and maybe bring back something to eat.

She had dreamed of a white wedding, including the groom in white tuxedo and white bowtie. He was handsome, of course, but as time went on, and two marriages went down the drain, she dreamed of just having someone who would come over for a night now and then. Lately, she didn't even dream that. She didn't even dream about the well-trained white dog. She wished now she had dreamed of something more substantial, like a real career, but like the wedding, a dream was a dream, and the fact was she was an unemployed woman in her thirties in a car with bad tires that leaned to the right, and in the passenger seat was a woman with a wandering eye, a good throwing arm, and an uncertain personality, was far from what she had expected.

WHEN it was solid night, Jane discovered the headlights worked but the bright switch did not, and her arms and hands had nearly become numb from wrestling the wheel for a few hours. The air conditioner was moaning like an old woman about to pass some breakfast tacos and a fried pie.

"I think we ought to stop somewhere and get a bite to eat, fill the tank and go on. Maybe we can find a Safe-Mart parking lot to sleep in. Done it myself once," Henry said. Her voice had been silent for so long it was almost as if the radio had suddenly been turned on. It startled Jane.

"I went there to get a light bulb, and ended up having to buy four, and other items, and when I got back in the car, it wouldn't start. It was late and I didn't know what to do, so I just sacked out in the back seat and slept. Next morning there was a snotnosed kid smearing his goo and looking in the window. His mother yelling out, 'Davy, get away from there.' I got the car going all right the next day. Found out I was trying to start it with my house key. It fit right in the key slot. It was an easy mistake to make. I think a few cans of Colt 45 out of the Walmart cooler section might have affected my judgment."

"I'm sure," Jane said.

"He was tall for his age."

"Who?"

"The snot nosed kid.

It was late when they came to a town, saw a Safe-Mart and whipped in there, and decided to buy something to eat. But after looking around and enjoying the air-conditioning, they decided nothing was jumping out at them, so they drove and found a Dairy Queen. They bought DQ Dudes, which were a bit overcooked, but more to their taste.

Jane spent her time eating the Dude thinking all the while she should have bought a prepared salad from Walmart. She told herself that after this meal she would have to back off that business so as to keep her ass from wrestling out of her dress at the wedding.

Ronnie was going to shit her wedding cake on the preacher when she saw that she was showing up, and looking like she had just come from a classy bar and lounge. She hoped Ronnie's husband would look her over, and she liked to imagine him losing his stuff and saying something like, "Wow, your sis is sure swell looking."

However, it was highly unlikely that Ronnie's soon-to-be husband would notice much outside of how much beer there was at home in the refrigerator and who was winning at NASCAR. As well as what day it was that Ronnie's check showed up. That would be his laser focus.

None of this was as important as the wedding gift she needed to come up with for Ronnie, and how much she could spend on it. Ronnie was registered somewhere, but Jane had forgotten the card, and only had the address for the wedding written down on a piece of paper in her shoe with her money. She was reasonably sure that a toaster had been on her sister's list, and she determined that a toaster was her target.

After the DQ Dude, they went back to Save-Mart and sat in the parking lot for a few minutes, parked between a big truck and the racks for the shopping baskets. The truck was one of the tall ones, so high up you damn near needed an elevator to bring you down from the seats.

"Why does anyone need a truck like that?" Henry said, and though it wasn't a subject that Jane considered a lot, it was an opening.

"I haven't any idea," she said.

"Yeah, me neither," Henry said. "I can drive a truck like that, though. I drove dozers and graters when I worked on county road crews, but I dug up a water main and they fired me. I worked on a farm using a loader to move cow manure from a big ole barn, but when I carried it out to the fields so they could distribute it for growing hay, I ran through a barb wire fence and they fired me for that. I miss the free lunch we got on the farm. Lady sure could cook."

Jane waited for a follow up until it became uncomfortable, and finally they figured out sleeping arrangements, which meant Henry got the larger back seat, and she got the front seat. They didn't have any cover or pillows, so Jane got out and pulled her bag of panties and bra out of the trunk and tucked it under her head, and with the windows cracked just a little, they decided to turn in.

Despite the sweat inducing heat, Jane felt as if she had slept a little when a mosquito buzzing around her ear woke her up. She slapped at it a few times, but the mosquito proved to have excellent evasive maneuvers.

Jane sat up and smacked her lips. She was as thirsty as a carp on holiday in the Sahara. From the back seat she could hear Henry snoring. It was like listening to a chainsaw gnawing its way through an oak stump.

Jane decided to go in the store and try and get some insect spray, a few odds and ends, including bottled water. She put her purse inside the bag she had under her head, as it was easier to carry than the purse, the strap of which had become worn and cut into her shoulder when it was well stocked with this and that, as it was now. When she got out of the car, the mosquito got out with her and followed her to the sliding Save-Mart doors. Jane slapped at it numerous times, but it continued to be elusive.

By the time Jane stepped into the Save-Mart air-conditioning, the heat-loving mosquito had abandoned her. She at least had that going for, that and the air-conditioning which was as brisk as an arctic wind.

She walked about pushing a basket and loaded her buggy with a dozen bottles of water encased in a plastic wrapper. She decided to spend a bit of her money on a couple of cheap pillows, and bought two on sale sheet sets. She figured they would make a nice cover and might even protect them from squadron attacks from mosquitoes, though she knew if they took a mind to it, they could suck blood right through a sheet. Technically, only Kevlar could prevent mosquito bites. With high hopes she bought some mosquito repellent.

A man who limped and wore an unneeded heavy coat and a hat with ear flaps started following her, and to lose him, she took a turn down the peanut butter and jelly aisle. But he followed her, and he was picking up speed, despite the limp. He came along as if one leg were on a pogo stick.

Jane took a hard right at the end of the aisle and went down the beer cooler section. This aisle appeared to increase his mobility, and he had caught up with her by the time she was about to turn left toward the dairy aisle. She could see a small cooler island of salads and potato salad ahead of her, and she thought she might circle that, and lose him, like a clever soldier dodging around a hill to elude the enemy.

This was not to be, because the man began to say, "Miss. Miss."

Although she felt she should ignore him, he sounded so plaintive, she stopped, decided what could go wrong here in the middle of Save-Mart? He has a limp and looks as if he could be blown over with a handheld battery-powered fan, and here she was a healthy, and scrappy, young woman (no emphasis on the young). Surely, she could defend herself adequately until the stock boy she saw placing bagged cheese on a rack nearby could come to her rescue, perhaps with a block of cheese as a weapon.

Of course, the stock boy looked only a little sturdier than the limping man, and far less motivated, so maybe that wasn't a good game plan, because the stock boy pushed his buggy, now bare of cheese, out of site.

Jane turned to keep a direct eyeball on the limping man, and she saw that he was carrying her bag, which she had brought in with her. It was the one with the panties and bra and her purse in it. She was certain she had placed it in the little loft of the buggy, but there the man was, carrying it, limping quickly, and holding it out toward her, calling, "Miss. Miss."

As he arrived, seemingly out of breath, he said, "I'm tuckered out."

"I see I lost my bag."

"Yes, ma'am, you did."

Jane studied his face, which looked as if it had been in an accident. It had the look of having caught on fire and the flames having been beat out with a cheese grater.

In that moment, Jane remembered leaving her bag unattended while she reached the pillows off a high shelf, and now that she recalled, she thought someone had paced by the buggy quickly, grabbing at the bag. If that was true, for the life of her, she couldn't figure why they would return it if they stole it. She also considered another thing. Besides her changes of underwear in the big bag, and the purse, all her money and credit cards in her shoe, perhaps another ploy was in action.

These suspicions were further aroused when the man gave her an insincere smile, and said, "You move fast for a small woman."

"I'm not that small or that fast."

"When you're a cripple, a turtle has a sprightly pace about it."

"I'm sorry you're a cripple." Is was all Jane could think to say.

"Well, you dropped the bag some rows back, and I had to work to catch up with you, and thank you for that. I'm sorry I'm a cripple too, by the way."

"I didn't mean for that to sound the way it did."

Limping Man held up a hand. "Not at all. No offense taken. It's a truth and not open to discussion. I am a cripple."

"You know, not actually. You get around pretty good. It's not like you're on crutches or in a wheelchair or nothing and I noticed you were making pretty good time."

"Excellent observation."

"Well, thanks for the bag," Jane said, but the man kept hold of it, close to his body, like a colostomy bag.

"I ain't doing this for nothing in way of a reward. Not really."

"Not really?"

"Well, I believe in doing a kindness because it is a kindness, just as my old mother used to tell me. Bless her long dead heart. I could use a bit of money, though, now that you mention it, just a bit. I appreciate the offer. If you can spare it."

"I'm afraid I can't, but I surely do appreciate you finding and returning my bag."

The man didn't move to return it. "So, nothing?"

"Yes. I apologize, but I'm on a really tight budget."

"Are you? Do I look like a spendthrift? Do I look like dollar bills are falling out of my pockets? Compared to you anyway?"

"Well, maybe I can spare a dollar."

"A dollar. What do you think I am? A child in need of money so I can ride the horsey out front?"

"There isn't a horsey out front."

"I mean a mechanical one."

"There isn't one of those either."

"Well, if there was."

"You know what I think," Jane said. "I think you stole my bag, and then when you saw there wasn't anything in it worth stealing, you decided to return it to see if you could make something on a reward."

"You think that, do you?"

"I do, and don't try and run away from me. I think I can catch you."

At that moment Jane became aware of a whirling sound, and glanced toward its source. It was one of those motorized carts that stores provided for those who were unable to get around, meaning primarily lazy assholes who were invalided not by nature, but by an inability to stay away from chips, cookies, candy bars and cake, and a dislike of any form of physical motivation.

The man in the chair spilled out of it in places. He wore overalls and no shirt and his chest was gray and hairy. His head was bald, except for a sort of toiletbowl ring of poorly dyed hair that ran over his ears and around to the back of his head. He had a sweet face turned pink by the exhaustion of working the lever on the cart. He wore diabetes socks and no shoes. He had a candy bar in his hand, the paper peeled back, and he was snacking on that. In his lap there was a long sausage encased in plastic; the sausage was almost as thick as an athlete's ankle.

He rolled up close, almost between her and the limper. The fat man saw her looking at the candy bar in his hand, the sausage in his lap, and he said, "I'm going to pay for these things later. I keep the wrappers so they can scan it."

"He ain't gonna pay for nothing," the limper said.

"Ignore him," the fat man said. "He hasn't a spot of manners. What seems to be the problem here?"

"Now you're a cop," said the limper.

"Just protecting my end of the store," said the fat man.

"Your end? You ain't got no end, Terry. You ain't got no store."

"It's an unlicensed job, I admit. But, I am, madame, what you might call the unofficial mayor of the West End of Save-Mart."

"He ain't no mayor of shit," the limper said. "He's just a big fat asshole that rides around in that chair and eats what he wants off the racks. Even has one of those grabbers on a stick he uses to get stuff that's way up high. You can see it right there. It folds in the middle."

Terry, to help the limper out, pulled it out of a little bag on the side of his car and held it up. Jane could see that it was folded in the middle.

"He takes stuff all the time, and ain't nobody does nothing, on account of he's in with the night watchman. I think they suck each other off in the storage room."

Jane turned red. "I'd just like to have my bag."

"Say you would," said the limper. "Well, there's people in Hell want ice water too, but you think they're gonna get it?"

There was a buzz, and Terry rolled his motorized cart onto the limper's foot.

The limper screamed. It was pretty loud. Jane thought there would be a rush of folks to see, but no one showed up.

There was music going on the speakers and she noted it was a really bad version of a Beatles song sung by some people who were definitely not the Beatles; perhaps a barbershop choir that couldn't find a barber shop, but had found twenty-five dollars apiece to record cheaply. Except for that, and the limper breathing heavily and whimpering from time to time, the store seemed empty, which, due to the time of the morning, mostly was.

"Get off my foot, fat ass," the limper said. "You're breaking it."

The fat man did not roll the cart off of the limper's foot. The limper had sat down on the floor and his foot was at an arched angle under the wheel of the cart. His sadly demolished face was red enough to be radioactive. He was whimpering like a car-struck dog.

"I had to roll over his other foot last week," said Terry. "It was self-defense."

"Wasn't no such thing," the limper said. "He did it out of spite."

"I don't think so," Terry said.

"Grief's sake," Jane said. "Get off his foot."

The fat man finished off the candy bar and let the wrapper fall in his lap, then he wiped his fingers on his overalls with precision. "I sometimes have to have a little something come late at night to get my sugar up."

Jane hadn't asked about the candy bar, but she had a feeling Terry liked to keep his sugar up constantly.

Terry took a deep breath and backed the wheel off the limper's foot.

The man jerked his foot back after the wheel moved, and made some jagged noises. "I don't think I can get up," he said.

"That's all right," said Terry, the mayor of Save-Mart West. "Stay down there and hand me the bag."

Limper hesitated.

Terry touched the switch on his cart, made it hum and roll forward a bit.

"Okay, damn it," said the limper. "Here it is," and he handed it to Terry.

Terry took it and lay it in his lap, covering the sausage, and technically covering his other sausage as well.

Terry looked inside the bag.

"Hey, that's private stuff," Jane said.

"Panties," Terry said as he moved his plump fingers throughout the bag. "What a colorful and stringy assortment."

"And mine."

"There's a wallet too."

"With nothing in it," said the limper.

"You did look through my stuff."

"Just to see if I might find your name to look you up and return it."

"You may not have known my name, but you knew who I was. You followed me, hoping to make a buck, and you stole the bag in the first place."

"Don't make me call the security guard," Terry said. "Now get up and go on."

The limper made quite a production of rolling on his stomach and using his arms to hold him up. He moved on his hands and knees to a counter with open six packs of beer on it, clutched that and used it to help himself to his feet. When he was standing, he hopped around and looked at Jane and Terry.

The limper held up a finger, said, "The world will rue the day when the milk of human kindness was drained from the souls of the living, and the milk was replaced with vinegar and bile. So, said Jesus."

"He did not," Terry said. "You made that quote up. Now go on or I'll run you down."

The limper took a bottle of beer from the open six pack, screwed off the lid and tossed the lid on the floor and took a deep swig out of the bottle of beer, then put it back where he got it. He reached in his pocket and pulled out a pair of black panties that Jane recognized as one of her own. He had snuck it from the bag.

He dangled them in the air for a moment, made a production of slipping them over his head in such a way that one eye and half of his mouth was visible. His nose was under the material and appeared to be a small penis nesting inside.

"That's mine," Jane said.

The limper sucked at the material, pulling part of it into his mouth. He made a loud slurping noise. His tongue darted around the edge of the panties and licked the air like a snake, then darted back into its hole.

"You still want these panties back?" he said.

"Nope," Jane said.

"Shall I run him down?" Terry said.

"No, that's quite all right."

"You can keep this on your mind," the limper said. "I get home tonight, I'm going to do something in these that will give me pleasure."

The thought of whatever that was caused Jane to wrinkle her face and feel a bubbling in her stomach.

"Don't worry," Terry said. "He hasn't got a home. He does what he does he'll have to do it in the warehouse bathroom. He lives inside a box in the store's attic."

"That doesn't make me feel any better," Jane said.

The limper still had the panties over his head, and was looking at them with his one eye, which glistened, possibly due to it starting to water. He raised one hand and slowly lifted his middle finger.

"I bid you both, adieu. And fuck you, Terry."

The limper turned his back toward them, and began to move down the aisle, hanging onto the shelf for support.

"I could catch him from behind, when he's not looking, run smack over him. Back over him a couple times."

"Quite all right," Jane said.

When the limper was about halfway down the aisle, he let go of the shelf and began to move more comfortably and rapidly, like a slightly wounded soldier trying to find a fox hole.

"I just ran over his toes," Terry said. "Both times. Week before, and tonight. He likes to put on and play the poor mouth. His people had money, and he inherited it when they died. Bought himself a little used car place. I don't think he ever sold a car. Moved down to lawn mowers, but that didn't last either. They weren't even the riding kind. Push mowers. He was behind the times. He ran through his inheritance like crap through a goose, not selling anything, buying big, shiny automobiles, expensive booze, cheap women, and song."

"Where did he buy the song?"

"It's an expression, dear."

SIX

JANE paid for the water, pillows, a few odds and ends like granola bars, panty liners, and the mosquito repellant, which she placed in her panty bag with her small hand bag, on the way out. She hated to pause and pull the credit card with her money from inside her shoe. Her hiding place had been revealed. Terry tried to appear as if he were looking up at the overhead rows of lights, perhaps to see if a neon needed changing, but she saw him eyeing her reaching the card from her shoe. The money was highly visible from where Terry sat.

With her shoe back on, pushing a shopping cart, Terry rolled along with her toward the exit. A man fatter than Terry wearing a blue security guard shirt with the store logo on it, and dark blue, too-short pants that had been unbuttoned at the top to accommodate a large belly, met them at the door. His shoes were strained at the side and he had on highly visible Halloween socks that were black with orange jack-o-lanterns on them and were several months early for the holiday. He had a round face and the top of his head was shaved and there was a pink strip at the top as if he had had a skin peel. He had grown a small mustache that looked as if it were a borrowed eyebrow. His sleeves were rolled up to his elbow, and on his left forearm was a tattoo that was large and spaced in two lines of anemic blue print. It said IN REMEMBRANCE OF WILSON, BLACK FRIDAY.

"Hello, Mayor." The guard was so jovial he could have been auditioning for the role of Santa Claus at the office party.

"Hello, there," said Terry the Mayor. "How's it hanging? Oh, pardon. Lady present."

Terry looked at Jane for some kind of confirmation that his slip was okay. Nothing was forthcoming. She was ready to dart around them, out to the car, and as she made what she thought was an athletic move, she found Terry had immediately positioned the cart in front of her.

"I'll go out with you, and so will Tiny here," Terry said.

"It's because I'm not Tiny," Tiny said. "That's why they call me that."

"How clever."

"My brother was a hoot. He's the one started calling me that. I liked it better than Tooter-bug, which was what my mama called me. I thought that was my legal name for ten years. It's not. It's Millard."

"I can see how you might prefer it to either," Jane said.

A dark cloud of memory floated over Tiny's head. He couldn't have gotten the Santa job right then. Jane could see his face shift. His eyes drooped and he looked weepy.

Terry turned as solemn as a sinner in church. "Tiny's brother, Wilson, he got run over in a Black Friday stampede. He was minding the doors."

"It was usually my job," Tiny said. "But that day they had me working in the back to make sure no one tried to sneak in the back way or sneak back there after they were in and eat food they'd picked up. We workers, we have a snack back there now and then, but hell, we're underpaid."

"True," Terry said, "and being mayor isn't a financially rewarding job."

Terry held up the sausage for Tiny to see. "Overtime," he said, and laid it back in his lap.

Tiny was still lingering in the past. "They stomped him to death. Knocked the glass out of the front doors, and ran right over him. They tried to close down the store, but the shoppers weren't having it. They had to drag Wilson out to the curb to get him in the ambulance, and further injuries acquired there."

"Those shoppers really wanted those big plasma TVs," Terry said. "They were nice. TV came with 3-D glasses too, and not the cheap paper kind."

"It was a good sale all right," Tiny said. "Figure if Wilson was going to die, he'd like to think it was for a special sale item. He was dedicated to the store. Still, it hurts. See, I marked myself."

Tiny held up his arm with the tattoo on it. It was hard to read that way. "See."

"That's tough," Jane said, and tried to channel into her face as much empathy as she had that late at night for creepy strangers.

Tiny lowered his arm in a theatrical fashion, and stood still like a soldier at attention, his mind still on smashed glass doors and laboring crowds in search of large, cheap TVs, and probably good prices on cartons of generic brand sodas.

"Look here," Terry said. "Let us walk you out. There's hooligans that sometimes roam the lots when it's late like this."

"They find a lot of dropped items," Tiny said, "but sometimes they decide to take them from the shoppers."

Jane doubted there was an actual plague of criminal activity in the parking lot. She was suspicious, but decided to err on the side of the possibility. She figured she could outrun either of them if they became hostile. Especially Tiny, who wheezed along with them as they went through the automatic doors. Terry might have some good maneuvers on that cart, but out in the open she assumed she would have the advantage. Hell, she had leaped out of a car in the middle of the night after a marathon bout of love making, or something akin to it, and had run naked as an ancient Olympian down into the creek behind where the church then stood, through the woods, and to her house while the cops were still working their way out of their cars. She was so fast she had watched them through her living room window as they came up to the reverend, who was wearing his pants backwards. She remembered everything looked strange in the flashing blue and red lights of the cop cars. The reverend stood barefoot and wobbly as they approached.

There was a trashcan just inside the store, and Terry tossed the candy wrapper into it. The panty-licking limper was right. He hadn't planned to pay for the candy bar.

Jane attempted to move ahead of the two, and managed. They fell in line behind her. Still, they persisted all the way to the car.

Standing there, Jane attempted a few parting words.

"All right, then. I'm off."

"Wait just a moment," Terry said. "I have something to ask you."

He then turned to Tiny, formerly known as Tooter-bug, and said, "Cut you off a piece of that sausage there. You earned it."

"What did he do?" Jane said.

"Walked you and me out to your car, in case of hooligans. And he has bad feet. Did it anyway. Those dogs are bound to be barking, huh, Tiny."

Jane noticed that Tiny had tiny feet. His huge body was supported by peg-like legs and ridiculously small feet. The weight that he bore down on those feet had to be uncomfortable, but somehow Jane doubted he'd earned much, even a piece of stolen sausage.

Tiny took the sausage and was attempting to cut a piece of it off the end.

"Not too much now," Terry said. "That's supper."

Tiny grinned at him and worked a chunk off and peeled the plastic covering and dropped it in the parking lot.

Jane picked it up and held it. She hated littering.

Tiny began to gnaw at the sausage. "It's not as fresh as last time."

"They pretend they change out every day, but they don't. That's been there a week, but I try not to take the best."

The back door opened and Henry struggled out of the car, stood against the open door. "What the hell is going on?"

"They walked me out," Jane said.

"He rolled you out, and that one there, I bet he waddled you out."

"That's not very nice, Henry," Jane said.

"You assholes disperse. Not you Jane. You stay."

"That kind of talk could get you arrested," Tiny said.

"By a security guard," Henry said. "I don't think so. Come on, Jane, if we're not going to sleep, let's get on down the road."

Jane nodded, pushed the buggy to the trunk, used the key to open it up, and placed the items she had bought inside.

"Listen here," Terry said. "Which way are you going?"

"None of your business," Henry said.

"Oh, for heaven's sake, Henry," Jane said. "No harm. North. We're going north."

"Meaning up to the highway there, and straight on?"

"That's north," Henry said.

Terry nodded as if considering some strategic war maneuver. "I understand we surprised you lady, woke you up, but... What's wrong with your eye?"

"It's still sleeping," Henry said, touching the eyelid of her milky eye.

"I meant the other one," Terry said, and Tiny laughed, and then Terry snickered.

"Ever had your fucking riding cart turned over in the parking lot?"

"Oh, the cart's heavier than it looks. Sorry about the joke. Your eye, I hardly noticed. Listen. Let me make you a proposition. I'd like a ride home, and Tiny here, who usually gives me a ride, well, he's pulling the later shift. I don't currently have transportation, other than this motorized cart, and it's not made for long trips or highway riding. I might could catch a ride with someone else works here, but it's a busy time for the employees. All I need is for you to take me down the highway a piece, and then I live off that down a blacktop, then there's a little dirt road, and some trailers. I'm in the smallest one. Just help me load the cart in the trunk and I can show you the way."

"That cart won't fit in the trunk," Henry said. "Not even if Jane takes those pillows out."

"I was thinking we could tie it down. Tiny here could help load it."

"What with?" Henry said. "A forklift? Tiny looks barely capable of loading himself out of bed."

"I am going to call the police you keep talking like that," Terry said.

"I'll tell you stole that sausage," Jane said.

"Ah," Henry said. "Shoplifters."

"Another one in there got a pair of my panties and licked them."

"Don't forget I protected you from him," Terry said.

"Not exactly."

"Look, let's all make peace," Terry said.

"Wilson always said to be kind," Tiny said.

"Who the fuck is Wilson?" Henry said.

"He got ran over on Black Friday by customers," Jane said.

"Ran over?" Henry said.

"Not by a car," Jane said. "He got ran over by feet."

"I don't give a damn if it was by a truck. I don't know any Wilson, and I don't know either one of you. No ride. Come on, Jane."

Jane pushed the cart to one of the racks provided for them, shoved it down the metal bar lane and hastened back to the car, opened the door and stood there a moment.

Neither Terry or Tiny had moved from the rear of the automobile. They both were like sentinels in search of enemy tanks.

Henry had closed the back door and opened the passenger's side front door. She towered above the car. Jane thought, now that is one tall broad, taller than I even realized and she has shoulders as wide as the doors on an elephant barn.

"Better move your fat asses out from back there," Henry said, "or Jane will run you over."

"Would you do that, Jane?" Terry asked.

"I think so. Yeah."

"Come on, Jane," Henry said. "Show them your tire treads."

"I'm not moving," Terry said.

"Me, I'm going to go on back to the store," Tiny said, and began waddling away; it was almost too painful for Jane to watch him go.

"Get in the car, Jane. Let's go."

Jane and Henry climbed into the car and Jane started the engine.

Terry had not moved.

Jane started to back up. She could see the top of Terry's head in the tail lights, a red dome.

And then he moved. She glanced in the outside mirror on Henry's side, saw him motoring the cart in reverse, out of the way.

She backed out, observed Terry behind her, shooting her the finger.

She honked her horn and drove away.

SEVEN

NOT far out of the lot and onto the highway, Jane noticed the mosquito was in the car, perhaps having followed her from the parking lot. Maybe it was a different one, but she liked to imagine that it was the same, a mortal enemy unwilling to give up. She was Jane the Far Traveler, and the mosquito was actually a man who had a special suit that made him small and annoying.

She slapped at it a few times, but it continued to be quick and crafty, and only interested in her blood. The lobe of her left ear felt knotted from where it had bitten her. Henry was left undisturbed by it.

"Maybe calling them fat was mean," Jane said.

"Look, I'm fat. I know it. Were they fat?"

"I suppose."

"Were they, or weren't they?"

"Yes."

"Then they were fat, end of story."

"I noticed, of course, but it just seems mean to call them that to their face. And you're not fat, just big."

"If I say it behind their back they won't hear me. Besides, they made fun of my eye. Doesn't that count for some kind of retaliation?"

THEY proceeded for quite some distance, and then it began to rain. It was a vicious rain and Jane had to turn the windshield wipers on high to combat it. The rain was winning.

As she drove, bent over the wheel, trying to see through the great sheets of rain, Jane thought she could hear a voice inside her head, low and plaintive, the words were not quite perceived. Jane chalked it up to exhaustion and mosquito buzz.

But then Henry said, "You hear that? Sounds like someone talking inside a box."

Henry tilted her head to one side, then turned and looked over the back seat, through the rear windshield.

"Goddamn it."

"What?" Jane said, but before Henry could respond, Jane glanced in the rearview mirror. She saw at the rear of the car, something wet and shiny and shaped like an overturned cook pot. It would swing left and then right. Finally, it swung wide left, as if it were about to attempt to pass.

She recognized it then for what it was. A balding head.

"Motherfucker stole a ride," Henry said.

Jane glanced in the outside mirror, saw that it was Terry. His face was wet and pink and wide-eyed in the taillights.

He had swung wide left and was easy to see now. Jane could see that he had the grabber on a stick clutched in both hands, and was hanging onto it with all the desperation of a mountain climber who's footing has just been lost.

That made sense. Jane was driving over sixty miles an hour.

Terry swung back to the right rear of the car and momentarily out of sight, except for the shiny top of his head, coated in the glow of red taillights.

Instinctively, she slowed, and this decision sent Terry wheeling farther right, and then she heard him or the cart, or both, hit the back of the car, and then Terry swung back left again, visible in her outside wing mirror, and then the grabber snapped at the hinge and Terry crossed the highway in his cart, moving at amazing speed, right over the other lane. As he came to the edge of the road there was a spew of gravel, and before Jane could stop the car completely, she dimly saw the cart launch out over a drainage ditch and she saw Terry thrown from the cart, like an awkward and obese crash test dummy, still clutching the broken grabber stick.

He flew quite high, arched and went down and out of sight somewhere in or near the drainage ditch that ran on that side.

Henry had turned to put an arm on the back seat and look out at the rain.

"That takes care of him. Couple days to a week from now, someone collecting trash along this stretch will find what they think is a giant turd in overalls."

Jane put the car in park and cut the engine.

"I'm going to go look. He might be alive."

"If he is, get a tire tool out of the trunk and finish him off."

Jane pulled the keys out of the ignition and carried them with her, suspicioning that Henry might want to continue the trip without her. Jane got the little flashlight she carried out of her panty bag, and crossed the street.

When she came to where Terry had sailed off the road, she pointed her light around, looked down into the deep ditch and saw nothing, but past the ditch, out near a line of dark woods and a barbwire fence, Jane could see the cart dangling off the top strand of wire by one of its wheels, the other was spinning idly, like a carnival ride.

The cart was empty. On the ground there was a bunch of stuff that had fallen out of it. Including the sausage, lying by the fence like a horse's amputated penis.

Jane heard something moving in the woods, but didn't see it. An animal most likely. She doubted with even the kind of launch off Terry had had that he had made it that far, over the fence and into the depths of the woods. There'd be some kind of trail of broken limbs, he'd have done that. Maybe a leg would be draped across a tree branch.

Jane walked along the side of the road, probed the depths of the ditch with the flashlight, and finally, what had looked to her like an old rotting log moved and moaned. She edged over to a place in the ditch where she felt she could keep her footing and went down there.

Terry was lying on his back on top of some piles of water-washed leaves. His eyes were like little dark marbles in the beam of her flashlight. He was still clutching the broken grabber. The rain was falling down on his face and running in the ditch.

"Are you all right?"

"What do you think?" Terry said. He sounded like a man suffering severe constipation. "I got so high up they made a seat belt announcement. One thing, though. I can't feel my legs."

"Oh hell," Jane said.

"Little joke. I can't ever feel my legs."

"Is anything broken?"

There was a long pause.

"Oh, probably not. I had this hard ground to break my fall. You know, you ask for a little ride, and then you think, I'll grab on and let go when I get near my road, but you drive fast lady. I was beginning to think I'd have to wait for when you got to Henderson. Figured you might have to slow down for a light, stop sign, a deer crossing the road, and I could let go and shoot off to a bus station for a ticket back to town."

"Wasn't anyone asked you to grab on back there."

"You just going to leave me lying here in a ditch, a poor cripple?"

"Thinking about it. You aren't broken are you?"

"I don't know. You can set me up, we can see if my ass falls off, maybe a foot or something. I think the mud and water broke my fall some. Where's my cart and sausage?"

"In the woodline. Might as well let go of that stick. It's ruined."

"I'm going to keep it. Might be able to fix it up with some tape."

"What would fix it is throwing it away and buying another one."

Jane had bent down and was trying to set Terry up so he could rest his back against the far side of the ditch, but it was like trying to place a walrus in an easy chair.

"Wait here."

Jane climbed out of the ditch, crossed the road and got in the car, sat behind the wheel and looked across at Henry.

"He's alive."

"You come back for the tire tool?"

"I came back for help. He's heavy to move."

"So, he's alive?"

"Yep. I tried to set him up but he's heavy. The cart he was riding in is hanging from a barbwire fence."

Henry looked through the windshield at the slowly dying rain. "Couldn't we just find the sausage, leave it with him, tell him we'll call for help when we get to Henderson? We could make up our mind when we get there if we are really going to call."

"I don't think we can do that, Henry. I can't, anyway."

"I'm just trying to get to an eye doctor appointment."

"I'm just trying to go to a wedding."

Henry furrowed her brows, said, "Think he might die if we wait long enough?"

EIGHT

JANE and Henry went out in the mist that was left from the rain, and crossed the highway. Even as they went, the mist began to fade and the moon peeped out from behind a cloud.

Terry, who still lay turtle-like on his back, was silver and misty in the moonlight. As Jane's light hit him, he said, "So, I suppose you two find this pretty funny?"

"Can't speak for Jane, but I certainly do," Henry said.

"You are a cold woman," Terry said. "I noticed that right off."

"My only regret is you didn't hit that barbwire fence."

Jane nudged Henry and they found the place where Jane had gone down before and climbed into the ditch.

"You're lucky you landed in all this mud," Jane said.

"Oh, my luck abounds," Terry said.

They pulled under his shoulders and set him up so he had his back against the forest side of the ditch.

"Tonight," Terry said, "my generally pleasant disposition has been tried. I'm certain you were exceeding the speed limit. I hadn't counted on that. You looked to me like a law-abiding citizen."

"You were hanging onto the back of my car with a grabber stick, and you talk to her about the law," Henry said.

"I don't know there's a law against what I did, but speeding is certainly a crime that results in a large number of deaths yearly."

Jane, feeling there was no future in the conversation, climbed out of the ditch and tried to get the cart off the fence. It proved heavier than she expected. But by shaking the top wire, she finally managed to tumble it onto the ground on her side of the fence, but upside down.

A moment later Henry was there, helping her set it upright.

"You could still consider my idea," Henry said.

"What idea?"

"The tire tool."

"I might actually be thinking on it a little."

"Why don't we see if we can drag him out of the ditch, put him in the cart, and let him ride it home."

"He wouldn't reach home till after daybreak in that thing, maybe longer. Certainly longer. Battery might die."

"Sucks to be him."

IT took a long time and some strained muscles, but finally Jane and Henry dragged Terry out of the ditch and laid him beside the road. The cart was another matter, but eventually a lower level of the ditch was discovered, and they turned on the cart and Jane rode it up a slight incline and managed it to the side of the highway.

When they unified cart and Terry, another labor worthy of Hercules, Henry said, "If you get started now, you could be home...eventually. We can give you a bottle of water to take with you. I got a stick of chewing gum I'm willing to let go of."

Terry just stared at them.

"Two bottles," Henry said. "But that's it. Sip as you go and make it last. Hell, I'll throw in another stick of gum."

"You'd do that, wouldn't you?" Terry said. "Leave an old crippled man beside the road with a bottle of water and some chewing gum."

"Shit," Jane said. "All right, let's see what we can do. Come on."

Terry motored across the vacant highway and stopped his cart at the back of the car. Jane used the key to unlock the trunk, took out the goods she had bought, with Henry's help, and they put them on the rear passenger side floorboard and back seat.

Henry had a beach towel in the trunk, and she took that out and draped it over the back-driver's side. They had Terry motor to the open rear door, and then through a series of back-straining maneuvers, worked him into the back seat.

"Now, don't get off that towel," Henry said. "You're muddy as hell."

"Where might you think I would be going?" Terry said. "Just load up the cart and take me home, please."

"The cart, it won't fit," Henry said. "We'll have to leave it."

"Oh, no. You can't. I need it. My livelihood depends on it."

"You mean it helps you steal at Save-Mart," Jane said.

Terry didn't reply. He chose to look hurt that such an accusation had been made. His bottom lip sagged.

Jane sighed. She and Henry walked to the back of the car, and after several minutes, finally managed to cock the cart enough that its front wheels sat on the edge of the rear bumper. They pushed the cart, and with the wheels, it was easier than expected. They swung it around so that it fit in the trunk, though the top of it was pushing the trunk lid up higher than the lid wanted to go.

"We ride along with that thing in the back, we'll have to go slow to keep it from bouncing out," Henry said.

"Wait."

Jane went for her bag with the panties in it, brought it out of the car to the trunk. She pulled two pairs out of the bag. One pink one and one white. She tugged and broke the panties apart, and then she tugged some more. They were surprisingly strong.

Henry watched all of this with the concentration of a spy.

Jane tied the panties together with a small sheepshank knot learned from an Eagle Scout that wanted to impress her, and then she tied one end to the top of the trunk, and stretched the panty cloth as far as she could. It wasn't long enough. It required one more pair. She was down to two good pair.

"I hate the idea that I might have to wear stained panties for a day or two."

"Hell, I do it all the time," Henry said.

Jane managed to sheepshank the added pair of red panties to the previous, and finally the lid was bound down to a lock catch at the bottom of the trunk.

Climbing back into the car, Terry cleared his throat, and Henry leaned over the seat and glared at him.

"You know, I was thinking," Terry said. "Did either of you see my sausage."

"It was lying near the fence," Jane said.

"Would it be too much to ask for you to go get it? I'm feeling a might famished after all that struggle."

"You have got to be kidding," Henry said.

"No. I mean, you've helped this far. Is asking you to retrieve the sausage that enormous a task?"

"Fuck it," Jane said, got out of the car, crossed the highway and went across the ditch with her flashlight. She eventually saw the sausage lying near the fence. As she approached, there were two glowing eyes moving out of the woodline.

Jane paused and watched. A raccoon, who looked experienced and nothing but business, scuttled out of the trees and under the fence, took hold of the sausage in its small human-like hands. It stood up on its hind legs, clutching the sausage like a yule log. The raccoon eyed Jane with what she thought might be a dangerous attack mode look; for all she knew he was as rabid as Old Yeller.

After making its status understood, perhaps viewing her as a fellow night wanderer and providing her professional courtesy, it clamped its teeth down on the middle of the sausage, dropped back to the ground, and disappeared into the woods as quietly as smoke.

Jane climbed back up to the side of the road and stopped there as a large truck roared by, splashing her with water.

"Perfect," she said.

Back at the car, Jane climbed in behind the wheel. She said, "A raccoon got it."

"You can't say that for sure," Terry said.

"Actually, I can. I watched it take it into the woods."

"Damn. I was looking forward to that. Maybe we could go into town and go through a late-night drive-through, though I'll have to owe you."

"That's not happening," Jane said. "Right now, I wouldn't piss on you if you were on fire."

"She already ruined three good pairs of panties tonight," Henry said. "And look at her. She's soaking wet."

Terry cleared his throat, as if to make some life-changing announcement. "Actually, she's lost a fourth pair. Back at Save-Mart there's a man in there with a pair of black ones over his head."

"This is true," Jane said.

The mosquito buzzed her ear.

NINE

IT was a longer trek to the turn off than Terry implied, continually saying, "It's just a little bit farther."

The mosquito stayed with Jane all the way, not bothering Henry or Terry at all. The bug had found its target and was sticking to it. Jane spent so much time slapping and waving at it, Henry said, "Are you having some kind of rigor?"

"Mosquito."

"Isn't bothering me."

"Guess not, it's over here."

"If you eat right, insects don't bother you," Terry said. "Me, they don't bother."

"Wow," Henry said. "Just wow."

"Is it the greasy sausage or the cookies that keep them away?" Jane said, taking a wild swipe at the buzzing mosquito.

"That was a bit of divergence from my usual diet," Terry said.

"I doubt that," Henry said.

Eventually, with Terry in charge of navigation, they arrived on a worn gravel road with a lot of red clay poking through, and came to a small formerly white travel trailer (it was gray now) in the middle of a field with one tall post and night light on it. The light gave off a weepy-yellow glow and was swarmed by insects. The trailer looked to have once been in a fire. One of the windows was dark and there were smoke stains on the outside metal of the trailer. There was a precarious ramp that led up to the doorway, obviously built for Terry to enter the door. The trailer was lifted high off the ground on stacks of concrete blocks.

As if they had asked, Terry said, "I keep it up high like that, cause come rainy season, this place is like a soup. Not deep or nothing, but always damp as a well digger's ass."

The cart deboarded with greater ease than its boarding, and they wrestled Terry into it. He drove the rattling cart over a stretch of gravel, then gave it full throttle up the ramp. When he was nearly to the door, he stopped the cart, and it miraculously held position. Jane noted that there was a length of trim wood nailed down on the ramp and it was designed to catch the back wheel and hold it if the cart started to slip backwards.

"This is where I normally use my grabber to unlock the door, but I don't have one anymore."

Terry twisted in his chair to look back at Jane and Henry, as if they had planned all along to drag him down the highway, break his grabber, and send him flying into a ditch.

"For heaven's sake," Henry said, went up the ramp and tried to open the door. She couldn't budge it. She looked back at Terry.

"It isn't actually locked," he said. "There's a trick to it. Push in and lift up, then pull back, but don't let it lower itself or you'll have the same problem."

Henry did as Terry instructed, and the door opened. The odor from inside smelled like canned fish and sweat. It was close confines and dark.

Henry stepped aside on the ramp as Terry rode the rest of the way up and into the travel trailer. He turned on a light.

"Come on in," he said.

Henry went inside and Jane followed up the ramp and after her. The place was cluttered. There was a stove to the left beneath the smoky, dark window. There was a sink across the way with a window that looked out on the pasture, beyond which there was a line of pine trees. Most of the illumination from the pole light fell back there, like a little pool of soured honey.

There was a couch that went from wall to wall at the back, and there was a Lazy Boy chair that looked as if has been rescued from a flood, and there was a TV with a pair of rabbit ears on it. There was a DVD player and a stack of DVDs.

Jane picked one up. It was still encased in the plastic and had Save-Mart stamped on it. Most likely another free shopping spree by way of the now broken grabber.

"We can watch something if you like," Terry said.

"Nah," Henry said. "That's all right."

"Okay. I got you. I got a bed there in the back. You can have the couch and the chair, you want to catch a few winks."

"We ought to go on," Henry said.

"I don't know," Jane said. "Maybe a couple hours sleep wouldn't hurt me. It's been a long night, and that mosquito is out there waiting."

"He'll still be waiting later."

"I thought I might lower the windows and see if he flies out."

Terry snorted. "Out here, you open the windows, tomorrow that car will be filled with them, thick as wool on a sheep's ass. Nah, that wouldn't be good. Just nap here."

JANE got her panty bag and suitcase out of the car, and Henry took her suitcase. They brought them in and set them by the couch, which Henry commandeered, leaving Jane to the Lazy Boy, which Jane soon discovered smelled like her first husband's underwear, which on wash day always looked as if a fist-sized turd had exploded in the back end, and the front was stained with multiple ejaculations. This was only one of the reasons she had divorced him. Sloth, alcoholism, and a neighbor suggesting, most likely with accuracy, that he had trained their pet goat to back up to a wide-gauge fence so he could fuck it were also important considerations.

Terry produced a couple of afghans from the back that smelled only slightly better than the Lazy Boy, and brought those to them.

"That's all I got, but it's some kind of cover."

"Where's the bathroom?" Henry said.

"It shouldn't be hard to find," Terry said.

"I was just being polite."

"It's right down there, but I need to give you some instructions. Way you flush it is you take the back of the lid off and pull up the string. The handle isn't fastened to anything anymore, and you got to kind of lean to the left if you're going to be seated on the commode, because the right-side flooring is starting to go. Cheap plywood. You get too much weight on that side, well, you might go through the flooring. One last tip, once you flush, it takes damn near five minutes to fill up again, and sometimes longer. So, pace yourself. Oh, only the left side tap on the sink works, and there isn't any hot water. I got to get a new heater."

Henry started off toward where the bathroom door had to be, but found it was a closet. The bathroom door was across from it. When she disappeared inside, Terry said to Jane, "I get the impression she kind of likes me."

"You do?"

"I seen her giving me the eye."

"Which one?"

"The good one. There's something interesting about the way the other one wanders around."

"She's going to get that fixed."

"I see," he said, "even if she don't."

He chuckled a little at his own joke.

Henry came out of the bathroom and said, "You sure got to keep your mind on something besides your basic business in there, or you get a serious wobble."

"Warned you."

Jane was going about spreading the afghan over the Lazy Boy, and was considering a trip to the toilet, but was waiting until the suggested five minutes between flushes had passed.

She decided she would sleep in her clothes, and not her pair of white, footed pajamas with the brown teddy bears and red hearts on it. She didn't like the idea of maybe having to leave quickly in her pajamas. Terry's place struck her as a residence they might want to abandon abruptly.

Henry tossed her afghan on the couch and sat down and started taking her shoes off. She put them on the floor near the end of the couch where she planned to put her head, because there were a couple of couch pillows there. She tossed one of them to Jane, who put in on the Lazy Boy.

"You think it's been long enough between flushes?" Jane asked.

"I'd give it another minute or so," Terry said.

Terry wheeled with trained precision about his kitchen, pointing out the shelves where cans of sardines and crackers could be found if the munchies attacked in the night, and suggested that the milk in the fridge might want to be avoided, as it had curdled a bit. He claimed he knew how to make cheese out of it, and that's why he kept it like that, but Jane found this doubtful.

"I think one should live simply, don't you?" Terry said.

Henry looked about. "How simply?"

"Obviously, you haven't read *Siddhartha*," Terry said.

"You're right, I haven't."

"Henry Hesse. A writer for the educated, the thoughtful. He concluded that most of our unhappiness comes from wanting things we don't need."

"I'm figuring his overhead was small," Henry said. "Probably didn't have a shitter that was about to fall through the floor with him riding it."

"It's a philosophical book. I don't think anything will be gained tonight by a meaningful discussion if you aren't about to take it seriously. Hesse was quite wise. Reading him changed my life."

Terry waited to see if there was going to be a continuation of a discussion about Hesse, but neither Jane nor Henry were biting, so he threw in the philosophical towel.

"There's soda pops in there too, forgot to mention that. Save-Mart brand, but it tastes alright, though it's got kind of an afterbite and smells a bit like formaldehyde when it isn't cold. I recommend you drink it pretty quickly. Goes down better that way."

Terry looked around the room in search of any other important components that might need explanation. "Light switch is right there."

He pointed at the switch by the door.

"The hall lights?" Henry said. "You leave them on?"

"Normally, but I got me a flashlight and a nightlight in my room. It's a cute thing. A little plastic bear that glows blue, on account of the plastic is blue, and the light behind it shines through it and makes a blue light."

"Yep," Henry said. "Figured that."

"Well, I guess I ought to say goodnight," Terry said, but he didn't move his chair.

Jane took her ditty bag with her toothbrush and paste and shampoo in it, and went around Terry to the bathroom, and found the floor as described.

She went about her nightly ritual, brushed her teeth and put her hair back with a thick yellow band and tried to wash her face, but there wasn't any soap. She had a bar in her bag, and used that. The water had a smell like sulphur and it was tinted a brown color. She brushed her teeth, but only dampened her brush, and spat as much of the water out as she could manage.

When that was done, she went out and Terry was still there, explaining some of the fine points of the sink plumbing, which seemed to be as precarious as the toilet system. The floor on the right side of the sink was also a death trap.

"Good night then, Terry," Henry said. "We need sleep."

Terry was reluctant to close up shop, but Henry stared at him with her one good eye, which made a person all the more aware of the one that wasn't good. This went on for a goodly time, but finally Terry blinked and broke contact.

"Then sleep well," Terry said, spun the cart, rolled back to the recesses of his bedroom and closed the door.

"I hate that fat rat-fuck," Henry said.

TEN

JANE slipped over to the fridge, opened it and took a can of soda. Outside of the spoiled jug of milk, all Terry had was a case of Save-Mart soda.

Back at the Lazy Boy, Jane flicked off the light and drank the soda, sitting there, trying to figure what she could get her sister for her wedding that was within her budget. Henry had already put her face to the back of the couch and had the afghan stretched over her, but folded down at the shoulders.

With her voice muffled by the couch, Henry said, "This damn thing stinks worse than the rest of this place."

"Oh, you haven't sat in this chair yet. I think I have the winning furniture."

"Let's just sleep a short time if we can, and get the hell out of here."

"Good idea."

Jane finished the soda, leaned over the arm of the chair and placed it on the floor.

"Good night, Henry."

Henry didn't reply, except to let loose with a snore.

JANE found the Lazy Boy to be worn out and uncomfortable with springs that poked her in the butt, and the smell increased with the afghan spread over her, or perhaps it was the afghan. She rolled it off of her, then found she couldn't sleep without the covering. She had always been that way. Even in hot weather she liked to be covered with at least a light sheet. It made her feel snug and safe. She thought about all manner of unimportant stuff, including the name of the dog in *The Little Rascals*, the white pit bull with a black circle around its eye. What was that scamp's name? She gave up.

After a bit Jane slipped off to sleep, but it was a shallow and uncomfortable sleep, like knowing she was waiting on her own execution. It was a weird sort of dream, like she had done something horrible, and in the morning, she would be executed by being hanged with a length of her own panties sheep-shanked together. In the dream the panty noose hung from a suit hanger fastened to a rack above her. Her former boss from the laundry showed up wearing a clown suit. He said, "Put ketchup on them panties, it'll work better that way."

Whatever that meant. Dream people had unique logic.

She was walking out to the gallows, and she was almost to it, and she could see the panty noose hanging from the suit hanger, and out in the front row she could see her mother and father and sisters. They were laughing about something, and her sister was wearing a blood-red wedding gown. The other sisters had on what Jane assumed were matching bridesmaid dresses, and the dresses were ugly, made of burlap with white frilly sleeves of tissue paper and a trim of the same around the bottom of the hem.

She was being escorted by Terry. He was in his cart and it was rolling along and he had hold of her hand, leading her to the platform where the noose waited. The wheels on the motorized cart squeaked a little, like an agitated mouse. They seemed quite loud for a dream.

Gradually Jane opened her eyes to a squint, and almost up against the chair was Terry. He was framed by the hall light behind him. He had her wallet and Henry's in his lap and he was going through them with expert ease. Finding nothing in hers, of course, but she watched as he peeled dollars from Henry's wallet. He was carefully replacing the wallets to where he had nabbed them when Jane opened her eyes fully and observed him.

He didn't see her.

Jane said, "Find what you want?"

Terry startled, caused his cart to roll back a pace.

"Shit, you scared me. You should be careful."

"So, I'm at fault here? You're stealing from us. Or trying to."

"Look here," Terry said. "I was merely collecting a bit of rent money."

"What rent money?"

"You're staying here tonight, aren't you?"

"Why you bastard," Jane said.

Now Henry had come awake and thrown the afghan off and was on her feet.

"What the hell is going on?"

"I caught Terry here collecting rent money. That's what he says it is."

"Rent, huh?"

"You could call it that," Terry said.

Henry shook her head. "I don't think I will."

Jane reached out from the chair and turned on the light at the wall.

"I was going to put these back," Terry said, holding up both Jane and Henry's wallets.

"Without the money in them, I presume?" Henry said.

"Jane's wallet didn't have any money in it."

"That makes it alright then, huh?" Jane said.

"You can't say I stole anything, can you?"

"And my wallet?" Henry said.

"Kind of light. I got three dollars."

"That's because I keep my bigger money somewhere else, you piece of shit."

Jane admired this, as that was her own method.

Henry produced the paring knife from under the couch pillow.

"I keep this handy for just your sort," Henry said.

Terry rolled back a pace in his cart. "Whoa, now. Let's not start carving turkeys."

"Why not. I sure got one in mind."

"Petey," Jane said.

"What?" both Terry and Henry said.

"Dog on *The Little Rascals*. I just thought of his name. I was trying to remember it. It just came to me."

"Pit bull with the ring around his eye?" Terry said.

"I don't know his breed, but his name was Petey," Jane said.

"Goddamn, I used to watch them kids every Saturday morning," Terry said. "They were always into something. Always putting on a show."

"I watched too," Henry said. "But I liked the one about the horse best."

"What horse?" Terry said.

"It was an old show and had Peter Graves in it and a big white horse. Or maybe the horse was black."

"Sure he wasn't brown, or maybe a pinto pony?" Terry said. "I think you're making stuff up now."

"Fury. The horse's name was Fury," Jane said.

"That's it," Henry said.

"Well, we all had an active TV life," Terry said. "But I don't remember the horse."

"Tell you what we're going to do, Terry," Henry said. "As two ladies to a thief who all watched the same TV shows, except the horse one, which you missed, we're leaving here now, and as a professional courtesy to a fellow fan of *The Little Rascals*, we aren't going to kill you. So we are all out of nostalgia right now. No way a decent person can get any sleep here with a cripple going through our goods."

"That's not nice," Terry said.

"Wear the shoe if it fits," Henry said.

Jane made sure her bag was secure, and then Henry wrapped her goods up quickly, and then the ladies put on their shoes.

Terry watched all of this with his arms crossed.

"I would have expected the two of you to be nicer," he said.

"Life is just full of little disappointments," Henry said. "Give me the three dollars."

Terry reluctantly handed it over as if he were the one being robbed.

As they started to leave, Jane took hold of the can of soda, and carrying her panty and wallet bag looped over her arm, pulled her suitcase with her free hand.

"Where are you going with that soft drink?" Terry said.

"The car."

"That belongs here."

"I've already drank out of it," Jane said. "What are you going to do, save it for later? I might have a disease."

"I might want to chance it," Terry said. "I might want to pour the contents down the toilet and flush it."

"If you do," Henry said, "I advise you don't stand on the wrong side of it, or you'll find yourself going through your floor."

"You won't let that go, will you?"

"I'm taking the soda with me," Jane said.

"I don't think so," Terry said, and as Henry opened the door by lifting and pushing, and Jane followed her out, he tried to grab the can from Jane's grasp.

He reached too far and began to roll down the ramp in his cart. Henry and Jane both stepped aside. Jane maintained her grip on the soda.

"Shit," Terry said, and he went down the ramp rapidly and off the edge of it. His cart tumbled on the ground and he fell out. "Goddamn it, that's twice tonight."

Henry and Jane started out to the car, carrying their luggage.

"You're just going to leave me here?" Terry called out. "What if it rains?"

"You'll get wet," Henry said.

In the car, Jane and Henry looked through the windshield at Terry.

"We might ought to at least set him up in his cart," Jane said, placing the can of soda between her knees, her hands on the steering wheel.

But before a decision could be made, they saw Terry wobble to his feet and set his cart upright.

"That fat fuck," Henry said. "He could walk all along. He had us pull him out of that damn ditch like he was a sack of potatoes. I damn near pulled my back."

Terry rode the cart up the ramp and into his trailer home, spun the cart and looked out at them. He raised his middle finger at them.

Jane turned on the engine and the car lights and they backed out, leaving Terry in the open doorway, maintaining his one-gun salute.

ELEVEN

THE mosquito was still in the car.

Jane slapped at him for a while, but the bug hadn't lost any of its evasive moves. Finally, it wore down and settled on the inside of the windshield. Jane knew how it felt. She too was exhausted.

It was misting rain and Jane turned the windshield wipers on and listened to them beat time.

Henry said, "I'm so tired I could sleep on a bed of nails."

"We're going to have to get a motel room, like it or not."

"Fine by me. Damn. I still smell like Fat Terry's couch. I know it's mean, but I hope he leaves the stove on or something and burns up in there."

"That is mean."

"An acceptable alternative would be if the floor broke through in the toilet and he broke his leg when he fell through. I like to think of him lying out there for a few days, but someone coming along and discovering him just before death."

"And who would that be?"

"A water meter reader. What does it matter. I'm making it up."

"That's true," Jane said. "Maybe it could be a Jehovah's Witness."

"Oh, I like that, and say the Witness, he tells Terry he'll drag his fat ass out and get him to a doctor to set his leg if he'll convert. And Terry says no, so the Witness starts reading one of those shitty tracts they carry."

"Say it's a long tract," Jane said. "One of those that folds out two or three times like a big road map."

"Yeah. And the Witness reads every word. Slowly. And they got one of those Yankee accents. Stressed vowels, or maybe it's stressed bowels. I don't know. But the Witness talks like that."

"Or like Porky Pig."

"Oh, hell yeah. That's the ticket."

"We might as well imagine ants crawling on Terry while we're at it," Jane said. "And I wish the mosquito in the car was back there with him instead of in here with us. Sometimes I think it's going to drive me crazy. I got a swollen ear lobe where it bit me. I think it might be infected."

"Bit you? Does a mosquito have teeth?"

"Good point. I don't think so. Pretty sure they don't. But they stick you and suck your blood. This one got me on the shoulder and the back of the neck too."

Henry had become disinterested. "It doesn't bother me any."

THE rain became so thick the headlights and the wipers were not enough to improve vision. Everything was a blur of rain, crawling worms of water that covered the windshield.

"You're going to drive us off in a ditch," Henry said.

"You were driving, we'd already be in one."

At that very moment they could see neon lights poking through the rainfall. The sign read OTEL.

"It's a motel," Jane said.

"I didn't figure it was an Otel," Henry said.

Jane veered toward the light and managed to bump up onto the drive without plowing through the front of the motel. They pulled under an overhang near the door and stopped.

Henry rolled down her window, and they both looked out of it. From that viewpoint, the motel seemed far less inviting than before. The plate glass windows that weren't being washed by the rain due to being covered by the overhang were fly specked, and on the windowsills were some of the culprits themselves, dead and stiff. The front doors were glass and one of them had been taped heavily with duct tape where it was cracked in a large star pattern.

"I figure we got to have a look at it," Henry said. "I'm so tired my eyelids need truck jacks under them."

They left the car sitting there, and went inside. It was a small lobby. Actually, it was less a lobby and more a small tomb. The air-conditioning could be heard struggling in the air ducts and the check-in desk was dark and battered and the top of it was covered in cigarette ash and burns. The supplier of the ash was a skinny, dishwater blonde woman that looked as if she had been turned into jerked meat by a slow drying process. A cigarette dangled from her mouth like a loose tooth. She wasn't old, but the sun hadn't done her any favors, and her wrinkles were deep enough to irrigate rice. She had on a tank top and her bare arms were browned water-wings of flesh.

Since Jane and Henry's arrival, she had moved very little. She was much like a lizard in the desert, resting on a rock. She nodded at them.

"You have a room?" Jane asked.

"Got several. Some of them are fit to be in, and those are already occupied."

"What about the less fit ones?" Henry asked.

"Well, they're small. But then again, all the rooms are small. There isn't a free breakfast, and for that matter there isn't any breakfast, and there's no room service either. So don't call to have a toilet unclogged. All we can send you is hope."

"Kind of figured that," Henry said.

"We got maids, but they only come on Thursday, and this ain't Thursday. So you take a room as you find it. We don't do wake-up calls either, and the TV doesn't work in any of the rooms 'cause we don't have a hook-up, dish, or antenna. Some rooms don't even have a TV. We don't replace the stolen ones. In case you haven't noticed, not that many people stop here."

"With the hospitality you got, I find that hard to believe," Henry said.

"Yeah, it's a fucking mystery all right. Want a room, or not? Change the sheets ever Thursday unless someone throws up in a bed, or bleeds in it. Then I'll come around and do it, or the day girl, my daughter-in-law."

"That's a lot of things you don't have," Jane said.

"Yeah, well, what do you want for twenty-eight dollars a night? You're lucky if the goddamn room lamp works. Once this place was hopping, and nice too, but then the interstate cut through up the road, and the motels there took most of the business. That's where everyone crosses, so that's where they stop."

"Wow, you're really selling the place," Jane said.

"End of the year, I'm out of here. My Bobby died this year, and to tell you the truth, it was like someone had taken a goddamn millstone out from around my neck. I loved him, but that man was demanding, wanting his beer at just the right temperature, and wanting me to dress up like a maid and do him. I was busy all the time putting on outfits. Only thing he did around here was drink coffee. The one time he decided to do some work, the little motherfucker was trying to patch the roof and fell off. He died right beyond the overhang there. Fell, bounced off the edge and smacked the concrete. Damn, it looked like someone dropped a bucket of red paint. Sonofabitch couldn't wait until he had the roof finished. Nope. He fell before that and the hammer slipped away too, came down on top of him. It didn't do him any good or bad. He was already paddling his boat to hell. You know, he could sing a real good version of "I Saw the Wreck on the Highway, but I Never Saw Nobody Pray." Aside from that, he couldn't sing another song that didn't sound like "Old McDonald Had a Farm." Never could figure that. Seems you can sing one good, you could sing two. Wasn't the case. Soon as the insurance money gets cleared up, I'm buying a good car, putting Bobby's ashes in the trunk, or if I'm having a bad day, one of the shitters, and heading out of here."

"It's good to have a plan," Jane said.

"Damn right," the woman said.

"You got two beds?" Henry asked.

The clerk came back from considering her future, said, "Yeah. Towels ain't fresh. We don't wash them until Thursday."

"Thursday seems like a better day for us to show up," Jane said.

"Yeah, but it ain't Thursday," the clerk said.

"Do you have wi-fi?" Henry asked.

The clerk just looked at her.

"Just fucking with you," Henry said.

Jane turned and glanced out at the rain. It hadn't slacked a bit.

She looked at Henry.

Henry shrugged. "What the hell?"

IT was a room they had to drive around to, and the door to it was under a leaky roof, the one the clerk's husband had attempted to mend before his untimely demise.

The entire motel consisted of twenty-five or thirty rooms. It was the sort of thing Jane had heard her parents call a tourist court. Jane felt the cold water run down her collar and make a bee line down her backbone toward her ass. Perhaps the room was dry.

The key the clerk gave them was a large, old-fashioned metal key. Jane used it to unlock the room. The lock groaned, and the hinges squeaked when she pushed the door open. When she snapped on the light, the room turned a sickly baby-shit yellow. The two beds were small enough to have been dog beds. The floor was cracked cement. There was a small end table between the two beds and it barely had room to hold a shoddy looking lamp with a thick tan shade with horses on it. The wallpaper had cowboys and horses on it, some cattle.

"Yee-haw," Jane said.

"Goddamn it," Henry said. "We're at the gateway to hell."

Once inside with their luggage, they found that they took up most of the room.

"Only thing missing is a big fat stinky turd on the floor," Henry said.

Jane pushed her luggage between the bed and the wall. There was just enough room for it. She wandered into the bathroom. After a moment, she called out to Henry.

"Hey, Henry. I found that thing that was missing."

AFTER a bit of minor clean up, Jane and Henry dressed for bed. Jane was glad to be out of her clothes and into loose pajamas. Henry had already changed and climbed in bed and was hugging one of the thin pillows. Jane turned out the light and climbed into her bed and slipped between the somewhat slick feeling sheets.

"At least the bed doesn't stink as bad as Terry's couch," Henry said.

"Or his chair," Jane said.

"Do you believe in numerology?"

The question was as surprising to Jane as if she had suddenly had a brick dropped on her. "What?"

"You know, having your own number, either lucky or bad?"

"I don't think so… No. I don't."

"Me neither."

Jane considered. "Okay. You do believe, don't you?"

"Kind of. What I figure is I was born under a bad number, a bad sign, got given some bad juju at birth, or some such. I got the eye problem, and I'm big for a woman, and well, there's just a lot of stuff."

"You're all right."

"You don't really think that."

"I don't know exactly what I think. I'm not the luckiest gal in the world either."

"You look nice."

"So does a porcelain spittoon. But people spit in it."

"I don't know that people really use those much anymore."

"It was a figure of speech. I was trying to make a point. I never had trouble meeting men, but I had trouble keeping them, and frankly I didn't pick all that well to begin with."

Henry grew silent. Perhaps she wanted to talk about numerology some more. To start the conversation again, Jane said, "So what is your number?"

"It's the one that turns up bad. Seven. Did you notice the number of this bad room? Seven."

"Henry, all the rooms are bad. They could say Fred on the door, and they'd still be bad. That doesn't mean a thing."

"Okay. But seven keeps coming up in my life, time after time."

"Seven has to come up in your life, there are only nine numbers and a zero. You remember seven because you've made it important."

"My Social Security number has sevens in it."

"All sevens?"

"No."

"But you only count the sevens?"

"Yes. Because they're there."

"That doesn't make any sense. You've got a number you believe is important, so you see it everywhere, because it is everywhere. Like all the other numbers."

"Maybe."

"Astrology. You believe that too?"

"Sometimes. If it fits."

"Ha."

Henry laughed this time. "I guess I'm just a mess, Jane. I like to have something to believe, even if it's belief in a bad number. That doesn't seem to go with my personality, does it?"

"I don't know I'm all that versed in your personality. But I think we all believe certain bullshit. True love. Magic numbers, astrological signs. Maybe we have to. Or some of us have to. I met a man that wasn't worth the toilet paper to wipe his ass, and I insisted to myself that he was better than he was, and that what I was seeing daily was not the real him, like the real him was hiding in the bathroom."

"Using that toilet paper he wasn't worth."

"Exactly. My sister, the one who's wedding I'm going to. We're never going to be close, and I know that now. I've known it all along, but saying it now I know it's true."

"Why are you going then?"

"I was the one that went the wrong way, far as the family was concerned. They all got married about the time they got the first drop of blood in their underpants, and had kids right away. I got married, but I waited a while. And still fucked up. I got married again, and it was just another version of marriage one. I had a run of boyfriends that weren't all that hot either. I had all these dreams I was going to own my own shop—"

"What kind of shop?"

"Hell, I don't know. I just saw myself as a business woman. Turned out I was just someone wanted to be loved, by anyone. That's what my business was, and it was bad business."

"I can relate to that. My mama always treated me like shit. I used to be mad at my father for running off, but a few years later I hoped he had the wind at his back and wished he'd taken me with him. She thought my brother shit ambrosia and nectar, peed Holy Water. I was glad when he was dead and then I felt bad because I felt good about it. When we were kids, he always picked on me, treated me like shit. One day he had a rubber band and said, 'Bet I can put your eye out.' I said he couldn't, but he popped it, and it turned out he could. I later heard my mother say 'Not bad enough she's ugly as a toad, now she's a one-eyed toad.' This didn't exactly build my confidence. I had college money through hard work on a road crew. I drove dozers and such. Later did farm work with machinery. I had a knack. I was saving up my money. I was going to be... You'll like this. An eye doctor. I think I could have been dedicated as shit. I thought I didn't do that, maybe I'd be a surgeon. Later I thought a nurse, and finally I thought I might have a janitor business that cleaned the hospital. I was tripping over my dreams and hitting all the stairs on the way down. My mama had access to my bank account, the money I'd saved for college. She gave it all to a preacher, and then she married the preacher. The preacher run off with the church treasurer and part time lady wrestler. And she wasn't even any good at it. Always injured. Couldn't take a chair across the back worth a damn. Years later Mama gave her life savings to the preacher who had the church across from your house. I prefer numerology and astrology to those motherfuckers, I'll tell you that."

"I see," Jane said. "Listen. I got something to tell you. It relates to the preacher, but I feel as we're traveling companions, I need to get it off my chest."

"All right, then. Shoot."

"Where's the paring knife?"

"Under my pillow."

"I wonder if you wouldn't mind putting it in the end table drawer."

"It going to be that bad?"

"That depends on your interpretation."

Henry pulled the paring knife from under her pillow and put it in the drawer and closed it softly. "I can get to that pretty quick," she said.

Jane nodded, said, "Thing was, one night I was so lonely I was singing to my vagina, and thinking about the cucumbers in the refrigerator, if you know what I mean."

"You wanted a salad."

"That's good, Henry. So, I decide I'm going to wear my little black dress, which if I wear it much more will be a little frayed, gray dress. But it looks good on me. I put on my war paint and my elevator-fuck-me heels. I won't lie, I was trying to entice."

"You could save yourself a lot of money and time by just wearing a sign said, YOU WANT TO FUCK?"

"I know how cheap it sounds, but I'm sharing with you here, Henry. Giving you a piece of my life, honestly."

"Share on."

"So, I see this good-looking guy there, and he's drunker than a bear in a cider barrel, and before long we're talking. I don't remember about what. It was clear both of us were looking for a chance to get our boats sailed, and it was all just blah, blah, blah, and the next thing I know I'm in his car and we're out back of where that church was your mama had dealings with, and we're riding the storm, and then the cops show up. I was in track once, and I can run like a goddamn cheetah still. I was out of that car in my birthday suit, carrying my dress and shoes in my hand, and down into the creek so fast a starving rabbit hound couldn't have caught me. I got in my house without showing anyone anything, far as I know, and watched them arrest that fellow, who was the church's preacher."

"That was you," Henry said, sitting up in bed, looking over at her.

"I know. I just want to get that out there since we're traveling together. I didn't know him from a plumber or a land baron. I was just, as I said, getting my boat sailed. I felt like a tramp later, and had to take a taxi to the bar the next morning to get my car. I live with regret, Henry."

Henry was quiet for a long time. She seemed to be adding up events to see what number developed. Maybe something connected to numerology.

"Hell, girl. I don't blame you for that. You didn't know he was a one-eyed snake."

"But you seem so judgmental."

"Ha," Henry said. "Shit, I been so lonely sometimes that if it wasn't for the rotating shower head and a warm stream of water, I might have hung myself from the shower rod. Though my shower rod wouldn't hold enough weight for a mouse to hang itself with a shoe string."

"So we're good?"

"Did you ever see him again?"

"I didn't, and didn't want to. You know, here's something. The whole thing with the preacher, bad as it was, wasn't as bad as a doctor I dated. He had a special collection he showed me. He kept skins from circumcisions."

"Can you do that?"

"Not legally, and I didn't know he had done such a thing until we had been dating a few months, and then he decided to share his hobby with me. He liked to take those skins and use them to make wallets and such. He had a stack of them. Said they were going out as Christmas presents."

"Damn."

"I know. He wouldn't tell anyone what they were made out of. He said, for all they knew it was well treated calf skin, on account of the wallets were so soft. If he had been any prouder of his hobby, he would have to have been triplets. Night he showed me that I told him I remembered I forgot something in the oven, caught an Uber ride and went home, and that was it. I changed my phone number and the locks on the door. I guess he's still out there somewhere hustling dick skins and making wallets."

Henry pursed her lips and considered for a moment.

"If you were good at it, though, it would be a cheap way to fill up your Christmas list. I mean, I think since he could make a wallet, he might be able to make a purse, and if he got real determined, maybe he could make a pair of pants."

"Or a pair of shoes."

"Maybe some kind of hat bands, belts."

Jane laughed. "Yeah. Well, such is my life."

"I get you. All right. We're sharing, so let me tell you a secret about my family. I told you my brother put my eye out and he's dead, but here's the corker, the nitty-gritty. He was in a cult. He got in with this guy said he was like the new messiah, had a line of shit a mile long, and my brother, and about thirty other souls, swallowed it like it was melted chocolate. This nitwit was first a preacher with all the answers, and then he was the answer. He was rebirthed in human form, he said, only this time he looked like an overweight, bald guy with a psoriasis problem and tight pants, which believe me, I saw him a couple times in those skin tights, and that was not a plus. It was like seeing a peanut in shrinkwrap. He told them he had the powers of the universe. Turned out what he had was some kind of disease and died during a prayer meeting, or some such shit. He's telling them how he's cool beans, and the next thing they know he's biting carpet. George told me they kept his body around on the couch for a while, waiting for him to rise. He didn't. He kind of melted into the couch, and after a bit, started to stink. They had to give up on the rising, and finally the authorities were brought in. They bagged him up, hauled him off, and buried him in a pauper's grave. Maybe with the couch.

"Next thing George does, is he gets the idea he's the one that's the messiah, like maybe the soul of the dead preacher and would-be Jesus jumped into him.

"Congregation wasn't having it though. They deserted him and went on about being different kinds of losers, I figure. George, he decided he had to warn everyone the world was coming to an end, and he also needed money. He took to standing on a corner in Dallas with a sign that said THE END IS NEAR. CAN YOU SPARE SOME CHANGE?

"A lady driving an SUV ran over him, dragged him a ways under the car, and then she ran the SUV about halfway up a YIELD sign. Her Chihuahua had leaped into her lap and distracted her, and that's why she went off the road. Worse, I was told she planned to give George a dollar. They said what was left of him looked like a streak of strawberry jelly. He was a fool. I'm glad he's dead. My whole family is fools, and I just might be one too. Hell, Jane. Do you think you and me might be white trash?"

"I don't think so. But I can only speak for myself."

"You got to admit, I have one fucked up family."

"No argument. But that sign your brother had, pertaining to him, well, he was dead on. The end was near."

"That's true. I hadn't considered that."

"What's your biggest regret, Henry? Mine's not having children. Course, I needed someone who was a bit more than a breed bull, and that never happened. Get back home, I may get a dog, though. One of those you can carry around in a bag."

"My biggest regret is being me," Henry said, and her mood changed suddenly, shifted back to her more sullen self. "Now that we've shared, I'm going to put the paring knife back under my pillow."

Henry recovered the knife from the drawer.

Jane said, "One last thing. Why do you carry that all the time?"

"Because I hate everyone and don't trust anyone. And Jane, in the spirit of truthfulness, I don't trust you either. Turn off the lamp, will you?"

Jane turned off the lamp.

"Wait. For the record, what's your sign?" Henry said.

"Leo."

"Shit, we'll never get along. Good night."

TWELVE

NEXT morning it was still raining, and Henry was still sleeping. Jane slipped out quietly, went to the front desk by walking under dripping overhangs along the walk.

Inside, she found there was an attractive blond woman behind the desk. More of a girl, really. When Jane came to the desk, she could see the woman sitting in a chair behind it more clearly. She was heavily pregnant. Her body was skinny except for the belly, and it looked large and ready to explode beneath a tight-fitting T-shirt, which seemed like the wrong choice for a maternity blouse, as the shirt was thin and she wasn't wearing a bra. Her tits looked like two fried eggs with peanuts in the centers.

"I was wondering if you offered coffee," Jane said. "I was told no breakfast, but what about coffee?"

"I'm sorry, we don't. But since it's just you and me, you can come around and make some in our own pot."

"That would be nice. I have a traveling companion, and I'd like to bring her a cup too. You have cups, right?"

"They're Styrofoam."

"Better yet."

The pregnant girl got up, came around and opened the little half-door, led Jane to a small back room, which was obviously the room the owners, and this girl, who Jane assumed from things said last night, was the owner's daughter-in-law, used for their breaks.

There was a coffee pot on a table. The table had scars on it that appeared to have been made by a hammer. It was a good coffee machine, though. It was the kind with the little coffee pods, and unlike Henry's pods, these hadn't been used before.

Jane pulled a couple of Styrofoam cups from a plastic bag on the table, and some pods of creamer, as well as some sugar packets and a plastic spoon.

"You know, there's a couple of cinnamon rolls in the cabinet there. I'm not supposed to do it, but you can have them if you want. They're here, I'll eat them. They're wrapped in plastic. I'd as soon you take them. I'm hungry all the time. Nobody has played with them."

Jane was uncertain why anyone would want to play with a cinnamon roll, but she smiled, said, "That's nice of you."

The pregnant girl hustled up the packages of cinnamon rolls, and gave them to Jane.

"Thank you. That's sweet of you."

"Just protecting myself from them. So I don't eat everything in the house, you know. You and your friend are traveling together for fun?"

"We both have some place to go up north, so we're sharing the ride."

"I see. I'd love to get out and travel, even if it was driving down the road a piece. I'm just doing like everyone else in my family. Growing up, getting pregnant and raising kids by working as a beautician or waitress, or like me, working here. My husband works over at the aluminum chair plant. He's a lead man over there. Supposed to get some kind of raise. Right now, he just gets to go in the company's break room a little more often. It's not great, but one of my friends from high school, her husband works at the Walmart up the road a piece, pushes the shopping baskets back from the lot into the store. I guess we're better off than that. We want to buy a new car someday. My husband, Louis, he's got his eye on a Ford. Not one in particular, but when we got the money, he wants a Ford. He wants a pickup and I want some kind of car where we can carry the baby around easy. Right now my mother-in-law brings me to work. This job don't hardly pay nothing. And they're going to close this place soon. It's like around here in this town, you only got so many choices, and none of them are good. I did win a beautiful baby contest once. When I was little."

The girl added that last part in, Jane assumed, just in case she thought Jane might be thinking she was a recent entry, attempting to pass for an infant.

"I don't remember nothing about it, though. Mama always talks about it like it's something, and I guess it is pretty nice. Mama has the diabetes bad. My mother-in-law is nice, though. But since her husband fell off the roof, she talks about leaving a lot. What is it you're going to do up north?"

"I'm going to a wedding. Still have to pick the wedding gift. I'm thinking about getting a toaster."

"Oh, the four-bread toaster. One I'm talking is really special. It's called the Super Toaster, and if I had the money for it, that's what I would get. It's a little pricey, but you can do four pieces of toast at once, and if you like, it's got this timer on it, and you can set a clock on it so that the pieces come off at different times. You can always know what time it is by looking at the toaster. Has a little butter dispenser inside of it, and it sprays the toast with butter, and it has this other special feature. Toaster can be opened. You can get in there and clean out old crumbs and such. You don't do that, you get roaches in the toaster sometimes. Any toaster that'll happen. Me, I call them Roach Toasties. I don't eat them, but I call them that when they get cooked by the toaster. They have a smell. I will admit I've eaten bread toasted with them. I guess it was okay cause I didn't get sick. Course, I just got a regular toaster. You got to shake crumbs out of it. That's how I found out there were roaches in it, and I'd already eaten the toast. I might have eaten a lot of toast before I found them in there. I can't be sure. There were two of them. I wondered if they were family, like husband and wife, or brother and sister. Thinking about that, I felt a little sad. They were just doing roach stuff, then they got down in there, trying to make a home and eat bread crumbs, and one morning I pushed the lever down, and I cooked them. If I'd had that Super Toaster, I could just have opened it up easy and looked inside, and I'd have seen them. I'm telling you, go for the Super Toaster. It'll be worth it. Wish I'd spent the money on one instead of the crummy one I got. I got a sister, she's got one, and loves it. Me and her, we don't talk much. Mama said she went bad, run off or something. She took the toaster with her."

"Thanks for the suggestion."

Jane had learned that you had to speak fast and commandeer the conversation a little, because the girl spoke in long runs, and wasn't willing to give up the floor. If she paused for long, it was only to take a good breath and regroup. The smartest thing, Jane decided, was to disengage and escape.

Jane had been making coffee while they talked, and now she had the cups filled and was looking for a gap in the conversation through which to escape.

"Course, if those roaches had been alive when I shook the toaster, I'd probably have swept them off the counter onto the floor and stepped on them. I guess I'm not really about saving their lives all that much, you get right down to it. I'd rather be squashed than cooked, though. You can get one at Save-Mart. They just about got everything."

"Roaches?"

"No, they don't sell roaches. At least, I don't think so. But, I can't be sure. There might be some kind of need for them I don't know about. Fishing bait maybe. But I meant the Super Toaster."

"Well, thank you. Congratulations on the pregnancy."

"I'm not all that happy about it. My husband, he don't like me taking the pill. Says it ain't safe and ain't what God intended, but he won't wear a rubber either. Says it takes away from his pleasure, and god thinks a man ought to have his fun. It's in the bible."

"I don't think so," Jane said, then thought, well hell, maybe it is. Anything that might work in a woman's favor was generally absent of that so-called holy document.

"Now I got a bun in the oven, I can't think of nothing else to do with it but have it. It's not like I can loan it out for yard work. Not until it's twelve or so. Right now I got to carry it around, and that's all there is to it. I might have some more kids, but I think they should be spaced a bit, don't you?"

"Definitely. Good luck."

Jane, carrying the coffee and cinnamon rolls, left the break room and made her way to the front door, putting her back to it so she could hold the coffee and push the door with her butt. As the door opened, the girl called out.

"They talk funny up north. You got to really lend an ear to what they're saying, or you might end up owning a used car you got to finance."

Jane smiled as the glass door closed behind her. She turned and carried the coffee out to the sidewalk. She was moving fast, lest she end up having the girl tag along behind her telling her life story, and that of all her relatives dating back to a common ancestor that lived in the trees.

As she was walking under the overhang again, the rain coming down, she felt a chill that wasn't just from the wet and the wind. She recognized it as the horror of living so common a life that her death would be the end of all memory of her. She was only marginally doing more than that poor little girl behind the desk; that poor child had been given a green pea instead of a brain. Though, she was well versed on the Super Toaster, and Jane found her mind drawn to it as an actual wedding gift.

When she came to the room, she set the coffee on the sidewalk along with the rolls, and used her key to open the door.

THIRTEEN

ALL through the guzzling of her coffee and the chomping on the cinnamon roll, Henry had nothing to say, except for the roll being a bit stale and the coffee tasting like someone had drank ink and peed it into the cup.

It wasn't very good coffee, which was true, but Jane thought the cinnamon roll was pretty good, but maybe she had gotten a fresher package than the one Henry ended up with. Still, the way Henry spoke it made Jane feel as if she regretted talking last night, revealing so much about herself. A black cloud was hanging over her head, rolling thunder and cracking lightning.

In the bathroom, which Jane had called first dibs on, she managed what her mother used to call a bird bath, where you stripped off and stood at the sink and wiped yourself down with a wet rag.

Jane took off her bra and top, but left her blue jeans on, and used a damp washcloth, which looked a bit suspect and was stiff in her hands, to wipe under her arms and over her chest. She didn't use the cloth on her face, but washed it by tying her hair and splashing water on herself.

She looked in the specked mirror and decided her tits were a lot less perky than last year. She imagined them drifting south yearly, until they finally arrived at the Rio Grande. A lot of her felt a lot less perky than last year. She pulled her bra and top on, and returned to the bedroom and Henry, who was sitting on the bed.

Jane said, "Your turn."

About fifteen minutes later they were loaded up in the car and were blowing down the highway.

They went on like that, not talking, stopping now and again for a pee break or to buy a bottle of water, or in Henry's case, to buy a Snickers bar. She seemed to have a fifty-mile average on needing a Snickers. She took her time with them, nibbling delicately at each bar like a mouse.

As night set in, the gas tank needle began to nod precariously toward empty. They came to a road sign that had a fading white arrow painted on it, and above the arrow, GAS, SNACKS, RESTROOMS. There were holes in the sign where it had been peppered with a shotgun.

Jane took the turn and ended up traveling down a crumbling concrete road without street lights, and finally she saw one big light in the distance. It was the filling station. It was set off the road a piece, and except for the one light that was the gas station sign, advertising some unknown brand of gas, it was dimly lit, as if the owners didn't really want to sell gas, snacks, or have anyone pee in their restroom.

Jane pulled to the pumps and parked. She thought since she was driving, Henry might pump the gas, but Henry didn't move. She sat looking straight ahead as if on an astral journey.

Jane started to say something, but determined it wasn't worth it. She had to spend some time working herself out of her seat belt, minus any kind of suggestion or encouragement. She eventually worked herself loose from captivity, got out and saw the pumps were old, but they did have a slot for her gas card, on which she had left thirty-five dollars and thirteen cents. She filled the tank up and had money left over, enough for a meal and a cup of coffee, provided the meal was a bowl of cereal.

When she turned around, she saw that Henry was trudging from the car to the station, her purse hung over her shoulder by a strap that looked as if it belonged on a hunting rifle.

It seemed to Jane, that the next step, after a pee-stop, was to manage some money from Henry for gas, as their agreement had been a fifty-fifty split. At the moment the restroom, and then maybe a Co-Cola and a bag of peanuts were in order. It wasn't her favorite supper food, but right now she would be glad to have it. She sat back in the car, and casually pulled off her shoes and plucked a five-dollar bill loose, then made her way inside the filling station.

Once Jane was inside, she saw a man in overalls, wearing under it nothing more than his bare chest and a tattoo of a green monkey. The man gave her a look that made Jane think he was considering something. He was thin, a little bony even, and he wore a red gimme hat. It was so tight if it had been a smidgen tighter, it would have blown his ears off.

Jane politely asked where the Co-Colas were.

"In the cold section, just like any other gas station," the man said. "It ain't like this place is all that big."

He had a voice that could have cracked the block on a brand-new Chrysler.

Jane nodded, politely, secretly wishing him an early death, and found the cold section and pulled a Co-Cola out of it. It was in a large bottle and just said Coke on it. The last time she had actually seen the little bottles of Co-Cola had been in a novelty store that also carried nearly forgotten brands of candy bars and Dr. Pepper that was made in Dublin, Texas, with pure cane sugar. They also had peanut patties, which is about as close to pure sugar as you could get, and she had heard that one of her school mates, from her time in the third grade, had eaten one and died of a sugar high, though it wasn't something she could confirm. He was twenty-nine at the time, so Jane was doubtful that it would have been his first peanut patty. Maybe he could stand them better when he was younger. Maybe he had eaten too many. Maybe it was a bullshit story. Still, for no sound reason she could determine, she pondered it from time to time.

She rooted around the store for a few minutes and found a bag of peanuts that were old and withered, like dried peas. She put that back and examined a possible supper of beef jerky stick, but when she picked it up it had the consistency of leather even feeling it through the plastic cover. Finally, she settled on a bag of potato chips.

As she made her way to the counter, she saw a spinner rack like her parents used to talk about. It had dusty bags of toys so old they had to have been made in the previous century. There was a little cap gun outfit and there was a bag with a tomahawk and feathered headband and there was a pirate bag with a small plastic cutlass, a pirate eyepatch, a fold out paper version of a pirate's cocked hat, and there was a plastic treasure chest about the size of a snuff box with a slot at the top where you could drop in coins. The package even had a small parrot you could fasten to your shoulder with a clip. There were other combinations of outfits, princess and such, but she lost interest.

Jane placed her goods on the counter, and was about to pay for them, when Henry came out of the bathroom at the back.

"Henry," Jane said as Henry moved up beside her, "what say you pay for this, and I'll pay for the gas this time? That'll come out in your favor, me putting in a full tank of gas and all."

"How do I know it's in my favor?"

The man behind the counter said, "That's right, check on it. Someone can't find a soda pop in a store this size, might not can be trusted to count money."

"You stay out of it," Jane said.

"My store," said the man behind the counter.

Jane ignored him, said, "You pay for it, got me, and we'll call it even."

Green Monkey, as Jane had come to think of him, puckered his lips as if to spit, but let them de-pucker, and went about straightening a rack of cigarettes that didn't need straightening. He kept his eye on her, though, as if he feared she might pocket one of the fried chicken wings inside the so-called hot food counter which was covered by a long glass lid that was grease spattered from the inside, and fly-specked from the outside. Besides the chicken wings there was one lone worm of boudin that reminded her of the turd in the hotel restroom. The last time that glass had been wiped was when it was created and boxed to be shipped. It was obvious the only heat those delicacies were receiving was from a light bulb placed in a wire rack off to the side of the greasy metal pans that contained the filling station delicacies.

Jane waited for resistance, but none came. Henry began to work a change purse out of her larger purse, and proceeded to count change.

Jane went off to the bathroom, feeling confident she had accomplished a rare, small win.

When she came back Henry was no longer in the store, and the Coke and bag of chips lay on the counter.

"She said she didn't have the correct change, and you'd pay for it," Green Monkey said.

"She did, did she?"

"Yep."

Jane glanced out into the station lot.

Henry's car was gone.

AS Jane walked away from the counter, leaving the Coke and the chips, she saw three things almost at once. She determined that yes, Henry and her car were gone, and there was a man on the floor behind the counter, just off to the edge of her vision. She could see him through a break in a rack of chapsticks and funny animal design car sanitizers. He lay up against the wall, hog-tied with rope. His eyes were wide open and he was looking at her like a drowning man about to go down for the final time. The last thing she saw was Green Monkey's reflection in the glass door as he was coming up swiftly behind her, and even more swiftly, he brought a black bag down over her head and plunged her into darkness.

She tried to yell out, but sucked in a wad of cloth instead. And then she was hit in the head hard enough she went to her knees, and then she was hit again in the same spot and it was night time.

FOURTEEN

WHEN Jane came awake she was uncertain where she was, but she was being bounced and rattled along and she still had the hood over her head, and the air stunk of cow shit. Her hands were bound behind her back and her feet were tied together. Her banged head felt as if her brain was trying to crawl out of her ear.

"Goddamn it," Jane said to no one.

"Jane, is that you," Henry's voice said, and Jane could hear someone stirring beside her.

"Yes. Where the hell are we?"

"I don't know. I went outside and got nabbed. I hadn't been taken by surprise I would have used my paring knife on them."

"Do you still have it?"

"Yeah, but with my hands tied behind my back, it isn't much help."

"Where is it?"

"In the front of my dress. There's a pocket there."

"Don't it ever stick you?"

"Now and again, but just a little. It's mostly okay on account of it's in a cardboard folder."

"You owe me some gas money."

"Oh, for heaven's sakes. That's your concern right now?"

Jane slopped her head forward a few times and finally the bag began to slide. She bobbed her head until she had a worse headache than before, but finally the bag slipped off and she got a look at where she was.

It was a cattle car, and now that the bag was off her head, the stench of cow shit was stronger than before. Moonlight came through the close together slats on the sides of the long truck and the top and rear of the truck appeared to be covered with a tarp. As her eyes adjusted, she saw that there were piles of cow shit here and there, and in the far corner of the truck were several women with bags over their heads.

Closer examination proved there were two others on the other side of the truck, near the upraised tailgate. One of the women there said through her bag, with a slight Spanish accent, "Hope you like house work."

"Shit," Jane said. "We've been kidnapped."

"Who'd want us," Henry said from behind the bag.

Jane leaned forward and bit the bag on Henry's head and pulled it off.

"Damn," Henry said. "It really does stink in here."

"That paring knife, maybe I can get it with my teeth."

"You'll need long teeth. The pocket is deep."

"Let me have a try at it."

After determining where the pocket was, Jane tried to get her head into the pocket, and though it was a big pocket, a kind of kangaroo pouch, she couldn't manage it.

Finally, she bit the corner of the pocket with her teeth and pulled at it, ripping it loose on one side. She kept pulling until the pocket was more severely ripped, and then she got her teeth on the knife inside. She dropped the knife in her lap and took a breather.

"Now, here's the plan," Jane said. "Don't fuck it up."

"You expect I'll fuck it up?" Henry said.

"I expect the worst in general. Now, I'm going to swivel a bit, and you're going to turn so that you can use your hands behind you to get hold of it. Then, I'm going to swivel with my back to you, and you're going to cut at my ropes, then when I'm free, I'll cut you lose."

"I might cut your hands, your wrist."

"Don't do that."

"Taken under advisement."

Jane, unlike Henry, was wearing pants, so she had to keep her legs together to keep from having the knife fall between them. Henry swiveled and got her hands close to the knife.

"I think I turned on a cow turd," Henry said.

"Not to worry. We both smell like shit."

Henry got hold of the knife, managed the cardboard cover off, and then they switched back to back. Henry carefully went to work sawing the ropes. The knife wasn't dull, but it was meant for carrots, not a soundly wound rope, so it took some time. Both Jane and Henry were sweating like bishops in an orphanage at bed time, when the rope was cut through. Jane took the knife and cut her leg ropes free, and then she was able to make shorter work of Henry's bonds. After that, she moved about the bouncing truck pulling the bags off the other women's heads, cutting their bonds loose, then giving the knife back to Henry.

The other women were Hispanic, and one of them, a pretty, plump woman with eyes so black they were impossible to see in the night, said, "You gringas, you have wandered onto a bad path, same as us."

Jane recognized the woman's voice. She was the one who had mentioned house work before. She had a Mexican accent. Or maybe it was South American. Hell, Jane thought. What do I know about accents? Maybe she's from South Boston.

"My cousin, she got taken for this, and then she got loose, told me about it, and then they got her again, and now they got me. Neither of us should have gone to Jake's Country Lounge. Mama, she say, 'You girls are slow learners.' Mama was right."

"I'm not someone takes to house work," Henry said. "I mainly just do it if company is coming."

"Might as well get on board," the woman said, "'cause we will be doing lots of it. I can show you how to change a mop out quick."

"How do you know these are the same people that kidnapped your cousin?" Jane asked.

"'Cause my cousin, she says one has a tattoo monkey on his chest."

"Check," Jane said. "That's the one we saw in the filling station. I saw the real clerk, tied up, right before a bag went over my head and I got a couple of serious love taps. My head really hurts."

"I'm the cousin and I'm right over here," said a woman across the way in the far corner. She was wearing a pair of blue jeans and a dark top with fringe. She had on cowboy boots.

"Hey, cousin," Jane said. "How'd you escape the first time?"

"I wait until they sleep, then walked out. The guard they had, he was sleeping too. So, I'm okay a few months, but then, I had to go to the damn bar. I didn't learn a damn thing. I'm a creature of habit. I think, it don't happen twice. They got me out back the last time, and now I figure they moved on, you know. I walk the hall to the bathroom tonight, and bam, got a sack over my head and I'm carried off. I still need to pee."

"I was with her," said the original speaker, "and they nabbed me too. Mostly, they're trying to nab illegals. Me, I'm a citizen. My cousin, she's not."

"Way they got me," Henry said, "was out in the parking lot. They came out of nowhere. I could smell one. He smelled like Campbell's vegetable soup, I swear. Had I been alert, I'd have stuck a paring knife in their eyes."

"They gonna be mad, us being cut loose," said the cousin.

The other women didn't offer comments. Jane thought they acted as if they might not speak English. Maybe they were merely stunned. Jane knew she was, but nothing had ever stopped her from talking, except sleep.

"Think they're mad now," Henry said, "they're going to be madder when I stick them with this paring knife."

"They open the door, we jump them," Jane said. "We're not mice."

"No," said the woman who had spoken first, and who Jane could see more clearly now because there was light at the edge of the tarp and it fell across the woman's face. She was pretty and her eyes were dark as mine tunnels. "We're cleaning women now. No reason to kidnap mice. We are normal sized women, except for you—" This was directed at Henry, "and they don't care they leave us dead side the road we give them too much trouble. I hear rumors they got a corn field where they put bodies, and the corn there, it's way high. I think I could get used to dusting under the bed, it comes to that. I don't got no problem doing windows neither if the other side of the deal is the cornfield. And then they got the cruise ships too. Maybe we end up there. Hope you like water. Me, I can tolerate a little sea breeze, but can't swim."

"Well, we don't have to take it," Jane said. "We'll stand together."

"I don't know," Dark Eyes said. "I'm thinking we might not stand so good."

FIFTEEN

THE truck rattled on, and Jane began to think it was like the Flying Dutchman. That they would remain in it forever, the cursed driver looking for something always out of his reach. Perhaps the cows who belonged to the shit in the truck bed.

The cows had probably already been made into steaks and burgers, leather jackets and shoes for stores all over the U.S., maybe the world. Jane pondered on this, and felt bad for the cattle, but on the other hand, right now she could use a big juicy steak. She was famished.

Jane inched to the back of the truck, nearly falling due to the rough bouncing ride. The tarp was tied down with ropes at the tailgate. It was securely fastened, so it took some work to get it loose enough to take a peek outside.

What she saw was darkness and lots of tall trees. They were on a backroad. She considered trying to work the tarp loose some more, and then jumping. But the truck was moving fast. If she were to jump, she would most likely bend a leg behind her neck, maybe jam one up her ass, so it didn't seem as good a choice as first considered.

Still, dying from a jump might be the easy way out. Their captors were dangerous. They had tied up the clerk at that station, maybe to rob him, and then she and Henry came in, providing product for their other business. They had been in the wrong place, wrong time.

I just wanted to go to a goddamn wedding, Jane told herself, and here I am in a cattle truck heading into domestic servitude, and who knows what all else. God, she hoped she didn't get some kind of toilet detail.

DARK Eye's cousin held out as long as she could, ended up pulling down her pants, squatting and peeing in the corner of the truck while the other woman there made an intelligent move to the other side.

As she made her water, she said, "Not like I will stink things up worse."

This was true.

Another of the women, inspired by the cousin's actions, followed suit, then everyone had their pants up again and were waiting. Now Jane felt she had to pee, but she held the urge, not wanting to squat in front of folks, and in short time the need to pee passed; it had probably been psychological.

When the truck finally slowed down, Henry pulled her knife, and they prepared to push the tarp aside and jump. But when the tarp was gaped open the cattle car filled with car lights. A car had parked behind the truck.

Their planned escape was over before they could start it. Two men who looked capable of turning over the truck appeared and climbed in quick, grabbed at them, wheeled them around and jerked their arms behind their backs and put plastic ties on their wrists. They took Henry's knife from her as if she had been offering them a treat.

They were forced out of the truck, being helped down by another big man standing on the ground. Jane stood there stunned, staring into the car lights that were so bright she couldn't make out the car. Their escape plan had been brief, and Henry's knife threat had been useless.

A car door slammed, and Green Monkey walked into the headlights. He grinned at them.

"You thought you was going to run for it, didn't you? I seen how you was untied and such. Well, we got you tied up again. We got your asses."

"What is this about?" Jane said, due to a need to say something.

"It's about us making some money and you making it for us."

"House cleaning," Henry said.

Jane glanced at her. The light caught Henry's dead eye and made it look flat, like a coin.

"Them Mexicans are good for that. Two of them don't even speak English. They understand I'll whip your ass, though. You two, it's house cleaning of another sort. We got a foreign cruise ship that will buy your asses. One Eye there, we can maybe get her work at a haunted house set up or something."

"Fuck you," Henry said.

This tickled Green Monkey.

"Shit, I'd fuck anything. Even you."

Jane tried to catch Henry's one good eye, but she was on the wrong side. She wanted to try and signal to her to shut the hell up until they had the lay of the land, but that wasn't happening.

"You got to have a dick to fuck with, stubby," Henry said.

That was the straw that broke the Green Monkey's back. He leapt at her, pulled a pistol as he leapt, and hit her on the side of the head. Henry went to her knees.

"Goddamn bitch," Green Monkey said.

"That all you got," Henry said, and spat blood onto Green Monkey's well-scuffed shoes.

"I got plenty for you...you...you," Green Monkey seemed at a loss for words.

"Bitch, you're looking for bitch," Henry said.

"Bitch," Green Monkey said.

"There you go, nubby."

That got Henry kicked and knocked over onto her back.

"She's worth more if all her parts are working, even her mouth."

The whispery voice came from a woman climbing out of the car and coming around to the back of the truck. The headlights shone bright on her. She was four hundred pounds if she was an ounce. The woman waddled and wore a colorful Mumu decorated with an assortment of palm trees and parrots. The Mumu could have served as a circus tent for a large group of performers, a variety of elephant acts, and have room left over for a lion taming performance and a few active hamster wheels. She had a plastic tube in her nose that was attached to a bottle of oxygen racked on a little metal dolly with squeaking wheels. She had her hand on the handle of the dolly, and when she stopped to look at them, she leaned on the handle and the dolly for support. She nodded her head forward slightly. When she did, her long greasy hair fell on the sides of her face like damp seaweed. Jane felt that the last time she had washed it would have been a possible youthful baptism. Perhaps it was a fashion statement.

Carefully lifting her head, she made a step forward. It was so slow and deliberate a rat could have ran up her leg and kissed her ass and come run down the other leg and disappeared into the woods before her foot settled. She pulled the dolly of oxygen behind her. Her breath was ragged. She had a pie-shaped face, and her eyes were buried in it like raisins. She wore lipstick that appeared bloody in the headlights, as if she had just sucked the heart out of a dying deer. As frail as she looked, it was obvious she was the leader of this pack, the general of sorts.

"What you doing whacking on them?" said the woman, panting between words. "Don't scar up the merchandise."

One of the big men said, "Goober here got his feelings hurt."

"Don't call me Goober," said Green Monkey.

"That right," said the big woman, who Jane now thought of as General Mumu. "You get your itty-bitty feelings hurt, Goob?"

"She ought not to be talking what she was talking," Green Monkey said, nodding at Henry, who by this time was back on her feet, holding her hand to her head. Jane could see blood oozing between her fingers.

"That right?" General Mumu said, turned to one of the big men, said, "Bruce, will you give Goober one for the team."

"Ah, hell, Mama," Green Monkey said.

Bruce said, "Brace yourself, Goober."

"Shit," Green Monkey, A.K.A. Goober, said, and tried to tighten his stomach muscles.

Bruce moved swiftly for a big boy and uppercut Green Monkey a sharp one in the stomach, causing him to go to his knees.

General Mumu pulled her oxygen tank over to where Green Monkey was on his knees, looked down on him and said, "You don't hit the livestock. For being my own flesh and blood, you're so dumb a dead pig could add two and two quicker. Let me tell you, merchandise needs a lick, I'll have it done, not you. I might do it myself, but you, you keep your hands off. You ain't got no control, or common sense for that matter."

Jane wasn't entirely sure what the pig and arithmetic comment meant, but she made a mental point not to inquire. Some things might best remain a mystery.

The other women from the truck had remained silent, as if they were used to things like this, or understood them.

The worst thing Jane had expected was car trouble, a blown tire, running out of money, but this, not even a little.

Jane's eyes had become adjusted to the night and now she could see past the bug-swarmed headlights and could tell the car in front of them was none other than Henry's battered wreck.

"Now," said General Mumu, "let's get on to the transfer station."

The big men helped the Hispanic women climb up in the truck again, as if they were their dates and were loading them up for a hay ride. The tarp was tightened again. The men went around and got in the truck, cranked it up, and away they went, bumping and rumbling along. Jane and Henry stood in the truck's exhaust fumes, like birds in a poisonous cloud.

Green Monkey opened the back door of Henry's car and called to Jane to get in. She did, and without thinking, said "Thank you" as he held the door.

When she was inside, he slammed the door closed, and then Henry was told to get in on the other side. After that, General Mumu climbed in with her oxygen tank, and that shoved Henry and Jane together, practically put Henry in Jane's lap. General Mumu took up a lot of room. They had pushed the front seat up. No one sat in it. It was practically on the dashboard. General Mumu pulled a little pistol from somewhere and let it rest in her lap. Green Monkey drove. Only Green Monkey fastened his seat belt. He was cautious.

Had the General wanted to fasten hers, they'd have had to bring out an extension, maybe enough strap to swing from the peak of Mt. Everest.

General Mumu hummed as they went along, and then she turned silent, bored perhaps, said, "Y'all been watching *General Hospital?*"

"What?" Henry said.

"*General Hospital.* You watch it?"

"That shit still on?" Henry said.

"Ain't been the same since Doctor Tony left some years ago, but it's still got some good stories."

"Soap operas are for fucking morons," Henry said.

"No wonder Goober hit you."

"See, Mama. She had it coming."

"I'm starting to side with you."

"There are some perfectly good stories on *General Hospital*," Jane said, trying to lighten things up.

"That's right," General Mumu said. "There you go. Some of them women on there can be mean, can't they. I don't know nobody like that, do you? I mean, way they act, that stretches the truth some."

"I know one," Henry said.

That's when Jane noticed the big mosquito was buzzing around her ear again.

Perfect.

GREEN Monkey said, "You know this wheel cuts to the right, and the brakes ain't good?"

"Why don't you get that fixed for me?" Henry said.

"That ain't likely," Green Monkey said, turned on the radio and attempted to find a station. He finally located one that played seventies rock. It all sounded like screaming and guitar fuzz. Jane could practically see tight pants and bad acne through the radio. He turned it up loud, and it made the back of Jane's jaw ache. She tried to mentally block it out, but it was like trying to ignore a buzzsaw. General Mumu came to her aid.

"Cut that shit off. What the hell is that stuff? You listen to that? Goddamn, no wonder you're an idiot."

Goober reluctantly cut off the radio and sat sullen and hunched over the steering wheel for the rest of the drive.

"You try to give your family a little goddamn culture," General Mumu said, "and what do you get back, but that shit."

"I figure culture for you is a chicken fried steak and sweet tea in a fruit jar and a chocolate dingdong," Henry said.

"Now ain't you the cute one," General Mumu said.

"Culture is where you find it," Jane said. She was still attempting to soften the situation. She figured Green Monkey or General Mumu could go off their nut with the slightest provocation.

"I have you know, I try to avoid fried foods," General Mumu said.

"I don't think you're avoiding all that much," Henry said.

"I ought to shoot you right here in the car," General Mumu said. "I'll have you know, way I look, my troubles, I got a glandular problem, and I'm big boned."

"Your glandular problem is too many bags of Doritos and about a gallon and a half of sugar a day. And I'm figuring you can make a pie disappear faster than Houdini."

General Mumu made a noise in her throat like a lawn mower starting up.

"Something to that, Mama. You do like them chocolate ones with meringue," Green Monkey said.

"Shut up, Goober," General Mumu said.

"Just saying," Green Monkey said. "We get a pie, it don't last a day and ain't no one else gets a slice. Mama likes to take the whole thing, a glass, a plastic fork, and a gallon jug of milk into her bedroom and eat it while she watches her stories. You can hear that fork scraping that pie pan like a chicken scratching in gravel."

"I get peckish during the middle of the day, I'll have you know. It's the gland thing," General Mumu said.

"Is it?" Green Monkey said.

Now General Mumu had grown silent, and Green Monkey, likely sensing he might have gone too far and fearing upon arrival at their destination Bruce would be brought back into play, cleared his throat once, and pointed out a few deer standing alongside the road. The deer's eyes glowed in the headlights. Green Monkey offered a few remarks on the wildlife and how this location was great for hunters, and that he had seen alligators deeper in the woods along the river. He tried a few comments about the flora, and was saying how he was allergic to poison ivy, but when he realized he was speaking to dead air, he abruptly gave it up and stared straight ahead and drove.

General Mumu focused on the back of Green Monkey's head, as if considering a soft spot. She stared with great intensity and Jane thought that any moment she might decide to strike Green Monkey in the back of the head with her oxygen tank or the pistol. It was an idea that appealed to Jane, but she was thinking about the car running off the road, and hoped, in the end, General Mumu might have enough maternal instinct remaining that she wouldn't make that decision.

When they came to the transfer station, Jane was disappointed. She had hoped if she was going to be kidnapped and sold into slavery, there would at least be some interesting things to see and there would be clean restrooms and maybe even a snack bar.

The transfer station was a barn and a series of old, dark cattle stalls out to the side of it. Light leaked out of the cracks in the barn. There was a skip loader sitting next to the stalls. As the car lights bathed it, Jane could see that it was shiny yellow. Behind the loader and spreading out wide, leaking into the woods on the far side, was a moon-gleamed pond. Idly, she wondered if it was full of fish.

"That skip loader there is brand new," Green Monkey said. "We bury our own garbage with it, and just so you might give us trouble, might be something else buried out there, like say some asshole thought they could outsmart us."

Jane thought to herself, that in the case of Green Monkey and General Mumu, that might be about anyone they met.

Green Monkey parked in front of the barn, and Jane and Henry were nudged out of the car. With General Mumu halfway pointing the pistol at them, they were led to the barn door. When they got there, Green Monkey made with a secret knock and then there was a knock back from the other side. Green Monkey did a coded knock in return, and then General Mumu yelled out, "Open the goddamn door, for shit's sake."

A wispy woman opened the barn door, said, "We all agreed on a secret knock."

"You want me to knock your head with this here pistol, then keep standing there," General Mumu said, her bad mood still present due to the doubt of her glandular problems.

Wispy moved aside, not wishing to encourage a pistol knocking demonstration. Wispy had a pistol of her own, and she held it against the side of her leg, as if feeling for a holster.

"I was just being careful," Wispy said.

"Be careful not to rub me the wrong way, girl," General Mumu said. "That's what to be careful about."

General Mumu went on by dragging her oxygen tank, sucking air from the tube that stuck into her nose like she was battling the sniffles from a cold.

When she was out of distance of hearing, Wispy said, "What got up her butt?"

"She don't like people to know how much she likes pie," Green Monkey said. "Best to forget it. You know her ways."

The barn was well lit and there were a lot of people in there, men and women. The men were herding the women into open stalls and you could see chairs and tables and lights inside them. There were women applying makeup and fluffing the hair of the women being brought inside the stalls. The place smelled of conflicting perfumes and the mixture made Jane feel as if she were being assaulted with nerve gas. There was crying going on here and there, and now and again you could hear a man yell at the women to shut up.

Already fearful, Jane was now terrified, but determined not to show it. Henry merely looked pissed.

"You two are going to be dirt workers, not sex workers, so you go over here," Wispy said. "We don't like to start sex workers when they're old. It's the young ones men want."

Jane was uncertain if she should be pleased, or take that as an insult. She decided, either way, it was an insult.

Wispy looked as if she had been born under a cloud of meth. She might have once been pretty, but the goodness had been sucked out. Her face was sallow as candle wax and her teeth were blackened in spots. Jane somehow thought she looked familiar.

Jane and Henry were escorted to a section of the barn and brought into a small room with a slatted door. There were stools in the room and the floor was covered in ancient hay and there was the faint aroma of cows and cow shit, though Jane determined that might have been what she had acquired on her clothes during the truck ride. Green Monkey and Wispy came into the stall with them, both holding their pistols to their sides.

"Sit over yonder," Green Monkey said, nodding at the stools.

"Why don't you make us sit down," Henry said.

"I'm just aching to shoot your other eye out," Green Monkey said.

"I don't think you could hit an elephant in the ass with it tied to a post," Henry said.

"Let's sit," Jane said, and gently touched Henry's arm, navigating her to one of the stools.

They sat.

Green Monkey said, "I got something in the car here for ole One Eye. I'll be right back."

"I don't need flowers from you," Henry said.

Green Monkey snorted.

After he left, they sat and looked about, and Wispy sort of swung her body gently from side to side, as if enjoying music coming from somewhere.

"So, you girls seen any good movies lately," Wispy said.

"Go fuck yourself with a rake," Henry said.

"Now that's not nice. I'm just trying to make pleasant conversation."

"Go fuck yourself twice," Henry said.

"You're not polite," Wispy said.

"Die and get eaten by raccoons," Henry said.

Jane leaned over, said, "Maybe you should lighten up for the moment. These folks aren't civilized."

In response, Henry grew stiff and silent as a gargoyle on a cathedral.

"There's no need to be sullen," Wispy said. "Your friend is merely trying to keep up a good face."

Henry didn't have a response, and Jane was thankful for that.

Jane studied Wispy carefully. She said, "You have a sister?"

"I do. She's kind of uppity. I ain't seen her in ages. Why do you ask?"

"Just curious, I guess."

There was no doubt in Jane's mind that the pregnant girl at the motel was bound to be this girl's sister. They looked very much alike, except Wispy had been in too many pharmaceuticals.

Jane considered confirming the relationship, but decided it wasn't worth it. Wrong or right, it wouldn't change matters.

After a while, the barn door was opened. Jane could see through the slats. Jane saw that the women from the cattle truck were being brought in. All of them were directed to the other side of the room, except for the one woman she had spoken to first, Dark Eyes. In the light of the barn Jane could see she was a little older and world-weary looking than the others. She was brought over to them by one of the big men from the truck. He clutched her elbow and slipped her inside the stall, closed the slatted door and went away.

"We're done out of stools," Wispy said, waving the pistol around, smiling like she was meeting a girlfriend for lunch. "You'll have to stand or sit on the dirt. Hey, I seen you before."

"That's my cousin. We look alike. She's on the other side of the barn. You can go say hi to her if you want."

"Not right now," Wispy said.

The woman from the truck eyed Henry and Jane, nodded at them and leaned against the side of the stall with an expression that implied all the guts had been pulled out of her.

"How do you get a job like this?" Henry said to Wispy. "Something this sweet, someone have to die to open up a promotion?"

Wispy took the remark as an honest question. "Oh, I know someone on the staff."

The staff. Wow, thought Jane, just wow.

That's when Green Monkey came back carrying a package. He held it up. It was the pirate outfit from the filling station. Green Monkey tore it open and pulled out the eye patch, tossed it to Henry.

"Put that on, so I can quit trying to follow your dead eyeball rolling all over the damn place."

Henry let the patch strike against her and fall to the floor.

"You put that on, or I'll end it for you here," Green Monkey said. "I'm tired of your sass. You're got and you're got good, so you might as well embrace it."

"It don't pay well," Wispy said. "But meals are free."

Green Monkey tossed her the rest of the package. The cocked hat leaked out of the rip when it landed at Henry's feet.

Henry picked up the patch with a trembling hand, and put it on with all the speed of a dead tortoise. When it was in place, she let out a sigh and lifted her head.

"That's better," said Green Monkey. "You won't be scaring people."

"It does look pretty good," Wispy said.

"Well," Henry said, "can I have the plastic sword, hat and parrot that goes with it?"

SIXTEEN

SHORTLY after Green Monkey went away, Henry, perhaps as a fashion statement, had put on the cocked hat and fastened the parrot to her shoulder. The parrot set there at a jaunty angle. Its dyed feathers were bright and multi-colored, its beak was the hue of old horse teeth, its plastic-bead eyes were dark as the bottom of a coal mine, and even the light resting on them refused to make them shine.

Henry held up the plastic sword, said, "Arrrr, arrrr."

Dark Eyes giggled a little, but there was a sadness in it, like a dying woman remembering a fart joke just before breathing her last.

"You're silly," Wispy said.

Outside the stall they could hear crying and talking and hustling about. Jane could see movement through the gaps in the slats.

"How do you sleep at night?" Henry asked Wispy, lowering the little sword into her lap.

"A cup of warm milk, a good pillow, and I'm right out."

Jane thought, all I wanted to do was go to a wedding for spite, and now I'm going to be swabbing decks and wiping windows. She should have stayed home and found out if they were hiring at the dollar store across the street.

Wispy waved the pistol around said, "Might as well get used to it. There's winners and losers in this life, and you ladies are the losers. The cruise ship, it's South American, and don't no one hardly speaks English. Best just to go along with things. You don't do as they want, you might find yourself set off on some island somewhere, or in the ocean without a rubber duck. It's a tough thing to find out, that you're going to be cleaning rooms on a cruise ship, but I done it for three years before I got promoted. I went along with things, girls. That's what you got to do you want to make it in this business. Had I had better teeth, I'd have been on the hump line with those girls out there. Some of them men get on you, they're big and fat and it just crushes your guts out. It's quick money, but you don't get none of it, so you got to consider a cruise ship lets you travel, though you got to see what you see from the boat. That's the business, girls."

"Business," Henry said.

"That's what it is. I worked my way up. Fucked the right people, ones didn't care about good teeth but appreciated a sunny personality. I made the toilets shine, and the boss, the big lady, Miss Sue Ellen... You know, lady in the Mumu. I don't know her last name, which I guess is her idea to keep it that way... But Sue Ellen seen I wanted to better myself, and she made me an overseer. I get to drive the truck to Mexico sometimes. Off the coast of Mexico, that's where you catch the cruise ship. You got to know people and pay the right ones to make the border cross in the right place, and it's kind of scary first time or two, worrying about getting caught, but once you do it, you get used to it, and it's nothing then."

"The Mexicans should build a wall to keep us out," Henry said.

"Oh, that would cost a lot of money. If the U.S. builds the wall, and gets the money from Mexico, that's the way to go."

"You," Henry said, "are delusional."

"I don't know what that means exactly, but I'm taking it to be good," Wispy said. "So, thank you."

Jane thought she could hear a cosmic clock inside her head, and it was ticking down to a bad midnight. There wasn't anyone to come look for her, or even miss her. Who knew when her sisters would check on her? She usually got a birthday or Christmas card from them, and the cards were about as sincere as get-well cards from Jack the Ripper.

One day they might look up and wonder, What the hell ever happened to our sister? Oh well. She's probably died or run off with some car salesman.

She didn't have any friends either. By the time someone missed her for not paying her trailer payment or light bill, she'd be out at sea wiping the rims of toilets and pulling sheets off beds for the laundry. Maybe screwing a patron in the closet and looking for a promotion.

"I don't deserve this," Jane said aloud. She had no idea it was going to come out, but there it was, in the open, like a rabbit that had broken through a prickly brush pile only to find itself on a firing range.

"Yep, life isn't fair," Henry said, gently snapping the plastic cutlass in the dirt.

"That's the truth," Wispy said. "Last time something fair happened to me, I wrote it down. But I've lost it since and don't remember what it was."

"There was that promotion you told us about," Henry said.

"There you go. That was it."

"I hate everybody," Dark Eyes said.

QUITE a bit of time passed, and Jane was happy that Wispy, who ceaselessly waved her gun about like a toy, hadn't manage to shoot one of them by accident, let alone design.

Green Monkey came for them. He was carrying a roll of toilet paper. No one bothered to ask why. He said, "Y'all come on out now. Damn, woman. That eye patch and parrot look good on you. I don't think you need the cutlass though."

"Oh no. I got the pirate outfit, I'm going to have it all."

"You forgot the little treasure chest back there," Wispy said.

"I can let that go."

They followed Green Monkey out of the stall, and Wispy brought up the rear with her pistol. She was twirling it around her finger like a gun slinger, provided the gun slinger was arthritic.

The barn was full of people, mostly Hispanic, though the first thing Jane thought was Mexican. It was an idea from her youth, that if you saw someone Hispanic in Texas, they were Mexican.

Jane turned to the Hispanic lady with them, said, "You Mexican?"

"I'm a fucking U.S. citizen by way of Guatemalan parents."

"Well," Wispy said, picking up the conversation. "Does that mean you're Mexican?"

The woman looked defeated.

"Sure. Whatever. Say I'm from Pluto, you like."

"I didn't know there was a town in Mexico named that," Wispy said. "There's a cartoon dog, though. I used to watch him and Micky Mouse. And his girlfriend mouse. I don't know if they were shacking up or not. I can't remember her name, but she was cute and wore a big bow in her hair and I think a polka dot dress."

"Minnie," Green Monkey said. "Minnie Fucking Mouse."

"That don't seem right for a kid show," Wispy said. "I don't think that was it. I don't think that was her name."

WHEN they made their way through the crowd of women, young and middle-aged, many of them speaking in Spanish, Jane realized that not only had the women in the truck been captured along with them, there were at least a dozen others. There appeared to be a handful of overseers, counting Green Monkey and Wispy. They were running things by gun and intimidation.

General Mumu was now sitting in a motorized wheelchair, a Rascal, Jane thought. She had removed the plastic oxygen plug from her nose, and was smoking a cigarette like it was the last one that would ever be made. Every time she took a drag a large piece of the cigarette became ash.

She was watching over her kingdom, where women were being processed to go to wherever it was they planned to take them. For a moment Jane was thinking at least she was going to be on a cruise ship. She would get to see a piece of the world, but it was a thought that only lingered a moment. There was that whole slavery issue to mar it.

By the time Jane and her group arrived at the barn door, where Henry's car was parked, General Mumu's cigarette was gone and she was hastily replacing the oxygen plug in her nose. The tank that supplied the oxygen was secured to the back of the Rascal with clamps. She had rolled to the barn door and was unwrapping a Honey Bun from a sticky plastic package. If she was in any kind of hurry, she concealed it well.

"What the fuck is that on your shoulder, woman?" General Mumu said.

"A parrot," said Henry.

"I see that."

"Then why ask?" Henry said.

"I meant why are you wearing an eye patch and a fake parrot. And is that a plastic sword?"

"It is," Henry said. "I felt like a bit of role playing."

The Guatemalan lady snickered.

"You're going to end up in a ditch with some thrown away beer cans and used rubbers you keep up that smart mouth," General Mumu said. "I see it coming. I've dealt with your kind before, you know. And you, best quit laughing, or I'll make sure you get the Captain's cabin to clean. He pisses all over the place. Couldn't hit the center of the bowl if his pecker had a telescopic sight on it."

Henry was about to make a remark, but Jane gently nudged her elbow.

"I gave that shit to her," Green Monkey said. "I got tired of her eye wandering around. The parrot, hat and sword are her choice. I only insisted on the eye patch. There was a little treasure chest, too, but she left it."

"You know," Henry said, "I might as well ask this. Have you got any secretarial work for us, maybe a managerial position."

General Mumu eyed Henry for a long hard moment.

"Cruise ship seems fine for these three," General Mumu said between chomping bites of her Honey Bun. "I haven't changed my mind on that."

"Ain't no one thought you did," Green Monkey said.

"Good to stay clear on these matters," General Mumu said. "Be solid on a plan, otherwise they could end up at a place they can escape from too easy. Remember—"

"I know," said Green Monkey, "if they speak Spanish, they can stay. If they speak English they best go. Cruise ships sail on their own graveyard."

"That's right, always keep them stupid," General Mumu said. "And easy to dispose of."

Jane assumed she meant put English speakers with Spanish, and Spanish with English to isolate the captives more. For the first time, Jane was truly beginning to feel a weakening in her bones, a feeling that her life was finalized. A few years in the Caribbean on some foreign cruise ship full of paying customers who not only liked their rooms cleaned, but their ashes hauled, and her last stop would be Davy Jones' locker, floating down there beside Henry and her plastic parrot.

It was a long way from wanting to be a weather girl when she was a teenager. Goddamn math destroyed her dreams. Or maybe, she thought, it was just me that did that. A little harder study and I could have learned fractions, she decided.

As Jane was feeling reflective, General Mumu said, "We'll drive them down to the coast by car. I got business down there. We'll take their car, dump it later. Helga, you walk down with them, help get them loaded up, then you come on back and do your job."

"Yes, ma'am," Wispy said.

"Helga, huh?" Jane said.

"That's right. We use code names though. My name isn't Helga. It's Tammy."

"What the fuck, Tammy?" Green Monkey said. "Why have code names if you're going to say your real name?"

"Oh," Wispy said. "I wasn't supposed to say that, was I?"

"Shit," General Mumu said. "You are dumb as a cedar post, girl."

"Yes, ma'am. Sorry."

"It don't matter none right now, just don't tell them your last name."

"Yes ma'am."

"You mean to say," said Henry to General Mumu, "that your son isn't officially named Goober? It's a code name. Somehow, that disappoints."

General Mumu looked about, called Bruce over. Bruce came like he might be expecting to punch Green Monkey in the stomach again. General Mumu said, "Take this spick with you. She's gotten wound up with these two, but they don't go together. Find her a beaner job of some sort."

Bruce nodded. Dark Eyes looked back at them sadly, like an old dog that was being dropped off at the vet for the last time.

"Just go on now," said General Mumu, munching on the last of her Honey Bun, wadding the wrapper up and tossing it on the floor of the barn.

"IT'S such a nice night out," Wispy said as they went outside the barn.

"Go to hell," Henry said.

"That wasn't called for," said Wispy. "I was just trying to have a good attitude about things. That's what got me through the cruise ship years. I did my work and didn't grumble, and I was taken notice of. Ain't that right, Willy?"

"Goddamn it, Tammy," Green Monkey, also known as Willy said, and he waved his roll of toilet paper about.

"Oh, yeah," Wispy said. "I wasn't supposed to say that."

"Willy?" Henry said.

"I'm gonna be glad to get shed of you," Green Monkey said. "You make me nervous."

General Mumu yelled out to Bruce as he went away with Dark Eyes, "Give all them bitches a granola bar or something."

"She's gruff," Wispy said, "but she takes care of her people."

By the car, Henry noticed hers and Jane's goods had been set out of it. They were piled on the ground.

"What about our stuff?" Jane said.

"You ain't gonna need that shit," Green Monkey said. "We'll give it to Goodwill or something."

"More likely he'll bury it with the skip loader," Wispy said. "That's what he usually does. He loves riding on that thing."

General Mumu abandoned the Rascal and they all got in Henry's car, along with the oxygen tank. It was a tight fit, what with Wispy added to the mix. This time General Mumu sat up front with Green Monkey at the wheel, and in the back seat Jane sat on the right, Henry in the middle, and Wispy on the left side with her pistol still being waved about. At any moment there was a chance she might shoot anyone in the car, and if the window was open, maybe an innocent possum in the nearby woods, hell, a fish in the pond. You got the feeling with her major accidents were always but an inch away.

The car bounced along until they came to the horse stalls, and Green Monkey pulled up between them and the pond, near the skip loader. When he did, his mother, General Mumu, said, "What are you doing?"

"You want to know what I'm doing? That what you want to know?"

"I said so."

"I'm going to go over into that old horse stall and take a shit, that's what I'm going to do." He lifted up the roll of toilet paper. "You ought to get a goddamn toilet installed, much as we're out here."

"Damn, Goober. Get it over with then."

"Hell, call me Willy. Helga already has."

Green Monkey, as Jane preferred to think of him, got out of the car clutching his roll of toilet paper and walked around front of the car and strode toward one of the darkened horse stalls, a man on a mission. He opened the stall door and went inside and let it swing shut with a loud noise.

"It probably would be nice to have a toilet," Wispy said. "I got a tick the other day when I was squatting in the woods."

"How about a bidet?" General Mumu said.

"I'm not sure what that is, but I think a toilet and a plain bar of soap and a lavatory would be nice."

General Mumu took a deep breath and let it out. "I should have left you on the cruise ship."

The mosquito had found Jane again. Its buzzing in her ear sounded like a jumbo jet taking off. Jane was about to slap at it when Henry swung her arm and hit Wispy in the throat with the edge of the plastic cutlass, hard enough she was knocked back against the seat and one of her shoes flew off. Wispy gasped like an apple was hung in her throat. The gun dropped from her hand, fell on the floorboard, and Henry, avoiding Wispy's thrashing legs, lunged for it.

General Mumu jerked around, looked over the back seat, trying to lift her gun up, but Jane leaned across the seat and gave her a jab in the eyes with two fingers. She was surprised she did it. What she previously thought was wasted time watching The Three Stooges had paid off.

It caused General Mumu to jerk back and fire off a shot that went through the roof.

From the stall, they could hear Green Monkey yelling. "What's going on out there?"

General Mumu, with a speed that had before gone unnoticed, worked the car door open and succeeded in getting out with her oxygen tank. She was pulling it with one hand and holding her pistol in the other. She started yelling, "Murder, murder. They done gone crazy. I been poked in the goddamn eyes."

Henry and Jane clamored over Wispy and out of the car to the sound of her trying to get her breath while she clutched at her wounded throat. Outside the car Henry started waving her pistol around, the parrot wobbling on her shoulder as if trying to find a perfect place to perch. "Come get some," Henry said. "Come bite a bullet."

Jane, even under the circumstances, thought Henry was overly dramatic, and the eye patch and parrot added to that. Henry had abandoned the cutlass and had lost her cocked hat in the fracas.

Green Monkey yelled from the horse stall. "Get my ass wiped I'm going to shoot someone dead."

General Mumu could see better now, having survived the eye poke. She put the pistol against the roof of the car and snapped off two shots at Henry, neither of which hit her. One shot scraped a groove along the roof and went on past.

Jane ducked and General Mumu fired again, and so did Henry. Neither hit one another, but as Jane ducked down behind the car, she heard a flat smack behind her, turned and saw Green Monkey staggering outside the horse stall, his belt loose and dangling. He was holding the roll of toilet paper in one hand, his gun in the other. He dropped the gun but clutched the roll of paper.

Damn, thought Jane. Toilet paper must be dear out here.

Green Monkey put a hand to his tattoo and sat down like he was in a game of musical chairs. Darkness oozed between his fingers and down his chest and over his overalls.

"Fuck a duck," he said and fell on his side with his knees drawn up.

General Mumu yelled, "See what you bitches done made me do."

Jane poked her head up and looked through the right rear passenger window. Henry said, "Get back down."

Jane stayed where she was. She saw General Mumu had moved to the side of the car and was looking through the open, rear passenger side window. Jane could see her clearly because Wispy was leaned back in the seat coughing, trying to get her breath. She had her hands to her throat where Henry had hit her with the plastic cutlass.

"I see you," General Mumu said, as she bent down and looked across at Jane.

Wispy let out a breath, then took in a deep one, said, "Ah, I can breathe again." She smiled, dropped her hands from her throat and rocked forward as General Mumu snapped off a shot. The bullet hit Wispy in the head and there was a messy moment with what looked like strawberry jam splattered all over the inside of the car and against the rolled-up window on Jane's side.

Wispy's head was turned toward Jane now and her eyes were dull as two cheap marbles. General Mumu stuck the pistol in the window and fired again. The bullet clipped Wispy's ear and glass shattered on Jane's side, but Jane had been pulled down by Henry just in time. Glass rained down on Jane's neck like hail.

Jane looked under the car, saw General Mumu waddling back toward the front of it. She was trying to be stealthy, but the wheels on the oxygen tank rack made a squeaking noise.

Henry handed Jane the gun, said, "You hold onto this and shoot her if you can."

"What?" Jane said, but the gun was already in her hand, and Henry was racing around the rear of the car toward the skip loader.

Jane, not feeling lucky about a shootout, slid around to the rear of the car too. She could see through the rear glass that General Mumu was at the hood of the car and was about to fall over from exhaustion. She was using the car for support, breathing heavily.

The skip loader roared to life. Its lights were turned on.

"Get on up here," Henry said.

Jane rushed from the back of the car, and just before she reached the skip loader a bullet whistled by her close enough to make her hair fluff. She climbed up on the loader, crawled through the door Henry had thrown open. It was some distance up to that door, but Jane was up there fast as an electrified monkey. Jane sat next to Henry.

"They left the keys in it," Henry said. "Stupid shits."

With expert ability, Henry wheeled the front-end loader forward. It jerked, and then she was maneuvering it around the side of the car, moving to the back of it, away from General Mumu and the gun.

Jane saw that General Mumu had managed the driver's side door open, pushed the tank and rack inside, and was climbing in. She started the car up and began driving it forward. Jane could see her clearly as they came to the side of the car.

General Mumu stuck her head out of the driver's side window and yelled at them. "I hate you! I hate you!"

The General suddenly slapped at her ear and Jane knew the persistent mosquito had found a new victim, perhaps attracted to her because of all those sweets she ate.

When General Mumu slapped, she stomped down on the gas reflexively and lost control of the wheel. Either that, or the car went hard right on her, as it tended to do. It bumped over the edge of the pond and shot out into it a goodly distance. The nose of it tipped and water flowed inside the open and busted windows quickly.

Henry drove the loader so that it faced the pond. The car was going down at a slant. The lights of the loader shined through the rear window and they could see General Mumu struggling to climb over the seat, to get to the rear of the car and out of the rising water.

It was about as easy for General Mumu to get over that seat as it was for a harpooned whale to scale Everest. Jane saw a little black dot bouncing again and again against the rear windshield. That pesky mosquito.

Water filled the car as it ducked farther into the water. Jane saw General Mumu looking at them. Her face was crunched up like she was trying to pass a difficult fart and her dress flowed up around her like a colorful mushroom cloud. Wispy's hair floated up suddenly, long and blonde. Jane could see General Mumu gulping water like a giant guppy. Then General Mumu, the dead Wispy and the evil mosquito, slid into the dark of the pond with a loud gulping sound.

A moment later all that was left were the lights from the loader lying cold and gold on the rippling water.

SEVENTEEN

HENRY backed the skip loader out and turned it around.

"Those poor devils," Jane said.

"Those morons killed themselves."

After a moment of consideration, Jane said, "Well, I can truly say I don't miss the mosquito."

Henry was driving the loader lickity-split toward the barn. Jane had thought Henry wasn't kidding about being good with farm and road machinery. She could really operate the loader. This wasn't what really concerned her, however.

"There's men in there with guns," Jane said.

"Yep," Henry said.

Henry raised the blade, pointed the loader at the double barn doors. She ramped up the speed and smacked the door with a splintering impact.

The doors went flat and it was suddenly bright due to the interior lights. Bruce was standing right in front of them.

He turned and tried to run, dodge off to one side, but Henry caught his ankle with the rolling track and crushed his foot to the ground. Bruce screamed and lay flat on his stomach, beating his hands against the earth floor like he was trying to punish it.

A shot hit the lift and ricocheted off into the barn. There were screams, and women started running. The other two big ugly bastards began to run.

Women made a break for it, scattered like a frightened covey of quail. They came to the back doors and someone threw a latch and the doors opened into the night. Women and the big men rushed out the door as if in a fire drill. A large woman had found a board and she was pursuing the two big men. She was swift. She managed several whacks to the backs of their heads as they fled across the countryside, looping to the side to run around to the cattle truck.

By the time Henry had driven out into the open, the woman with the board had lost interest, and with the others, was running like a gazelle toward freedom.

The cattle truck could be heard roaring to life. As Henry turned the loader, they could see the truck moving toward the road that had brought them in. The truck swiftly became nothing more than taillights, an engine whine, and a grind of gears.

Dark Eyes ran toward them, waving her hands. Henry wound the loader down so fast it skip-jumped slightly. When it was paused, Jane opened the door, leaned out and gave Dark Eyes a hand, helped her up and inside.

"It's kind of cozy in here," Dark Eyes said.

"That way we can wiggle each other's man in the boat," Henry said.

"What?" Dark Eyes said.

"Just ignore her," Jane said. "It's vulgar."

"Oh, I get it," Dark Eyes said. "That's funny. But I don't want no one wiggling it for me unless I invite them, and I don't want to wiggle no one else's little man."

"Whatever," Henry said. "It will go un-wiggled."

It was then that Jane remembered their luggage and they drove back through the barn, now empty of people, and went along until they were out the front door and parked next to where Green Monkey had deposited their luggage. They hadn't seen Bruce in the barn, but now they saw him limping off into the woods using a slat from one of the horse stalls as a kind of crutch. He was making grunting sounds and running through an inventory of a sailor's vocabulary.

Henry fired a shot into the trees. It whistled through the leaves with a sound like someone stepping on fortune cookies. This made Bruce limp even faster. He disappeared into the shadowed treeline wraith-like, leaving behind him a stream of painful screams and sounds that might have been from a non-English language.

Jane climbed down from the skip loader, and Dark Eyes climbed down with her, helped her grab everything, then they scrambled back up, dragging the goods with them.

Henry drove them out of there, following the dirt road the cattle truck had entered and exited by. They never saw the truck. The big, tough, bad guys had panicked like someone had yelled snake on a kindergarten playground. They had driven out of there so fast there weren't even exhaust fumes.

Henry stopped the skip loader after a while, climbed down with the gun. She wiped it off using her dress. She picked up a stick and stuck it in the barrel, cocked it back and flung the gun into the woods.

When that was done, she returned to the loader and drove them away.

THE loader moved pretty fast, but not so fast as to drive along the highway. They drove on the side of the road. It was rough there and the lights bounced in front of them. After a while they saw colored lights in the distance.

Henry pulled over and stopped. They were about a quarter mile to the lights.

"Why here," Dark Eyes said.

"I'm sure you remember that this isn't my personal skip loader."

"Yeah," Jane said. "She doesn't even have a license."

"This is true," Henry said.

"You come this far," Dark Eyes said.

"We really don't want to arrive on a stolen skip loader."

"We could say we borrowed it," Dark Eyes said.

"Everyone out," Henry said.

Jane, Henry, and Dark Eyes abandoned their ride and Jane and Henry dragged their luggage along on its rollers and Dark Eyes helped with the rest of it. Pretty soon they saw they weren't at the edge of town at all, but had come to a liquor store situated well outside of it. It was adorned in neon red, blue and green lights. There was a lighted sign in the window that proclaimed Budweiser as the King of Beers. There was a red neon sign on the top of a metal pole near the highway and the sign read Bus Station. Now and then the sign blinked a little, as if it was considering sleep. There was a little aluminum hut next to the liquor store with the same sign on it, though not in neon. It was merely painted on the door. There were no lights behind the one window in the hut, and the door with the sign was locked with a padlock about the size of a big man's fist. There was a phone booth next to it with an open door and an actual phone was there, not ripped out like they often were these days. There was all manner of writing on the phone booth wall with instructions for this and that, mostly sex acts and racial bad mouthing.

The liquor store had three pickups and a car parked out front. All the trucks were Fords. The car was a Plymouth the color of a mouse's hide. The liquor store was open and doing a brisk business with the owners of the car and the trucks. A clutch of rednecks who probably had cold pizza at home to go with the beer they were buying, or maybe some nacho chips soon to be covered in microwaved Velveeta, stumbled out into the night carrying twelve packs under their arms. They waddled when they walked, like farm-raised ducks. They worked themselves and their twelve packs of beer into their pickup trucks and the one ancient Plymouth with tires so bald you could damn near see the air in them.

As Jane and Henry and Dark Eyes stood there deciding their next course of action, the Plymouth made a sound like a horse gagging, fired up, and puffed black smoke out of its tail pipe. The smoke swirled around and went up and shadowed the neon lights of the liquor store before coughing its way out of the parking lot and onto the highway. A semi-truck honked its horn at the Plymouth as it pulled out in front of it. The semi swerved and passed at such speed the Plymouth shook and there was enough wind from its passing to ruffle the women's hair. The Plymouth chugged on, and as it did, Jane noticed one of its taillights was out.

Inside the liquor store, they encountered the store clerk. He was behind the counter, a middle-aged man with severe love handles that made it look as if an anaconda was coiled around his hips. He wore an obvious toupee the color of Number Nine coal.

"When's the bus come through?" Henry asked. "Is there a schedule?"

"I don't work for the bus line," the man said. "People come in here and ask me that all the time, and that ain't my lookout. Bus line closed up its office out there long ago. It still comes through, but you got to talk to the bus driver about tickets and such."

"Do you possibly have a schedule?"

"I do."

The man didn't offer to show it to them.

"May we see it?" Jane asked.

The man moved so slowly Jane thought the next ice age might be in progress by the time he produced the schedule and placed it on the glass counter top as if the act was something he was being forced to do at gunpoint.

Jane glanced at it, passed it to Henry and Dark Eyes. Jane asked for three Co-Colas and three bags of peanuts for herself and her companions; the peanuts hung on racks behind the counter next to the soft drink container. The man had to get up to get the goods, and he went about his work as if he were a prisoner at a gulag. Liquor was everywhere, but the soft drinks and peanuts seemed to be under some kind of special protection.

Jane paid with money from her shoe and took the Co-Colas and peanuts and passed them around.

Dark Eyes said, "I ain't going nowhere. Reckon they don't take pocket lint for a ticket."

"But you got that smile," Henry said.

"You are not that funny, girl."

It was Henry's turn to study the schedule. She had to tilt her head a little to see it. "No routes north, so we're out, Jane."

"Is that supposed to be a parrot?" said the man behind the counter.

Henry reached up and touched the pirate parrot. She had forgotten about it, and her comrades had grown accustomed. The parrot had fallen over and was dangling off her shoulder.

"Damn. I forgot to feed him."

"That ain't a real parrot," the man behind the counter said. "How'd you lose your eye? I ain't never seen a woman with an eye patch before."

"I'm guessing you may not know a lot of women," Henry said. "Is that a toupee. Not that it looks like one."

The clerk frowned. "You can give me back my schedule and get out of my store."

Jane took the schedule from Henry and waved it above her head. "This schedule belongs to the bus line. You said yourself you don't work for them."

"I'm disabled. This here job is almost more than I can stand."

"Well, thank you for your service," Jane said.

"I wasn't in no war. I fell off a chair."

"I hope the chair is all right," Henry said.

Outside, at the edge of the store, the women sat on the ground with their backs against the store wall and studied the schedule some more, drinking their sodas. Dark Eyes poured her peanuts in her Co-Cola, and after watching her, and being reminded of doing that very same thing in her childhood, Jane drank her soda down a little more, then poured her bag of peanuts into it. Only Henry remained standard and ate her peanuts by first pouring them into her hand and popping them into her mouth.

Jane thought the salt and sweet mixed together was delicious. She had never had anything so good, though at that moment, she was so hungry she thought she might be able to eat roadkill off the highway, if there were napkins with it, of course.

"Where you wanting to go?" Jane asked Dark Eyes.

"I got cousins in Nacogdoches. I could go there. It's on the schedule."

"That's not an expensive ticket," Jane said.

"When you got nothing, it's expensive," Dark Eyes said.

"Tell you what," Jane said, "you tell me your name, and I'll buy the ticket to Nacogdoches. It says they stop here at midnight."

"Ilene."

"That's a pretty name," Jane said.

"So is Sue and Sophia, but that money you got is about all we got, except a bit I got stashed," Henry said.

"We got a little less now. Ilene is going home."

"Yeah, and I ain't one to think Sophia is that pretty a name," Ilene said.

Jane slipped off her shoe and gave Ilene enough for a ticket, then said, "And here's a little more for a sandwich and coffee when you get to Nacogdoches."

"You're too kind," Ilene said.

"Way too kind," Henry said.

"You know," Ilene said, "you really don't need that parrot."

Henry unfastened the dangling parrot and tossed it past the former bus station office and into the grass.

They waited at the corner of the liquor store, which closed down and left them with less light, but the neon on the store and on the bus station sign were still on. They leaned against the wall of the store, and Jane fell asleep until she was awakened by the sound of the bus coming. When it stopped it was with a hissing and a slight thumping noise.

The door opened and the bus driver got out. He was a big black man in a crisp blue bus driver uniform and he had a small ticket machine fastened to a cord that hung around his neck.

Jane got up and helped Ilene with the ticket.

The bus driver, when he realized Jane and Henry weren't going, said, "You ladies ought to not hang out here this late. Anything could happen."

"We got a ride coming," Jane said.

"It coming soon?"

"It is."

Ilene smiled at Jane and got on the bus.

"You take care of her, she's had a bad night," Jane said.

"You had for dinner what I had, I could really tell you about a bad night. My stomach feels like it's being eaten from the inside."

"Her night might have been a little more busy and worse than that."

"She'll be all right with me. You ladies stay safe. That is a lady over there, right?" He was nodding toward Henry who had remained leaning against the store wall.

"It sure is. Say, you got change for, say a five? I mean silver change."

He did, and he gave it to her, said, "Keep the five. That's out of my pocket."

"No need for that," Jane said.

"I know," he said, and got on the bus.

A moment later the bus clattered and hissed and then glided away.

EIGHTEEN

"YOU'VE spent some of the money we need, we're sitting against a bus station wall, and we don't have a car anymore," Henry said.

A slow realization seeped into Jane and she sat up stiff against the wall.

"Oh, shit. They find that car they'll trace it back to you. And it's got our fingerprints on it."

"Being underwater, it won't have much in the way of fingerprints, and I'm figuring if there were, they'd mostly find Fat Ass and Willy's finger prints, them driving it last. They'll figure there was some kind of shootout between them, cause in a way there was."

"But the car is registered to you."

"No, it isn't."

"How's that?"

"That's not my car."

Jane let that sink in.

"Whose car is it?"

"I'm not really sure. Mine wore out and I sold it for parts. I had a nice man come and get it and give me some money and haul it off. I had to walk to town and all. I didn't have a car and I didn't have a job, but I had that money, and I lived cheap."

Jane remembered the reused coffee pods and the hard as rock cookies.

"I was walking back from town one day, and seen this car sitting beside the road. I looked through the window, and the car keys were in it. I went on, but the next day I was walking to town, saw it was still there. The door was unlocked. I opened it, started up the car, and drove it home. I let it sit in the garage mostly, but no one came and got me and I didn't read nothing about a missing car in the papers, though a body was found near there and it was figured it was a fellow who was lovelorn and had gone out in the field and shot himself and fell down in a ditch. No one mentioned the car, but I think they were connected. If I remember right, guy who shot himself, his name was Fred. Or maybe it was Sam. I don't remember exactly. Anyway, he's dead and he wasn't using the car."

"Jesus, Henry. You're a thief."

"I wear many hats."

"Oh, shit. You had a dead man's car."

"I wouldn't worry. We don't have the car anymore. It's at the bottom of a pond. They pull it out, look it up, I think they'll figure it was that crew nabbed us that stole the car. It's kind of a win-win."

"Win-win? There are dead people back there."

"Yeah, and there are a bunch of captive folks that have gotten free and run off. That includes us."

"I'm thinking I ought to feel worse than I do. We left behind us three dead folks, as well as a deceased mosquito. My personal nemesis, I might add. The bug I don't miss. But hell, there were three people killed, Henry."

"They were all pests of a sort," Henry said. "And we didn't kill anybody. They done it all themselves."

"Jesus, Henry. You're a regular desperado."

"I merely stole a car and scared some people with a skip loader."

"Which proves my point."

"Guess it does, a little."

JANE had been considering calling the police, which was why she had asked for the change from the bus driver, and finally she made the decision to do it. She told Henry.

"Just leave us out of it," Henry said. "The cops are tricky, so you got to be careful what you say. And don't stay on the phone long. They might track us. They have devices."

Jane worried about devices, but she thought she could make the call quick. She went to the phone booth and laid out some quarters she had gotten from the bus driver.

She hesitated, came back to Henry who was still sitting against the wall.

"I don't know where to tell them to go."

"I saw a sign said we came out Farm to Market road 724 and onto highway 59. Tell them to go down that road, heading west about five miles and then turn by an old oak tree that has its limbs sawed off where it would hang over the highway. Turn on the other side of it and go down about as far as you think someone can yell and be heard, and there's a road there on the right, more like a trail, take that, and then they'll come up on the pond."

"As far as someone can yell and be heard?"

"We used to call it a hoot and a holler, which is how loud a hoot is followed by a holler. What distance you can hear the two back to back."

"If you say so."

Jane went back to the phone and put in some money, and dialed 911. She wasn't even sure what town she was close to. The voice that answered was as crisp as a potato chip.

"Emergency services."

Jane put a hand over her mouth and tried to talk deep and through her fingers.

"There's been a station attendant robbed and tied up off Highway 59."

"We know about that. He worked himself loose. Who are you now? I can't hear you very well."

Jane ignored the question. "There's also been a shootout and a bunch of people were being held captive where it happened, but they've ran off now."

"What? I can't hear you. Sounds like you got your hand over your mouth."

Jane removed her hand but kept the deep voice. She repeated what she said before. "They run a car off in the water out there. Not on purpose, but some folks were shot first and then there was one that was drowned in the car."

It was all Jane could do not to mention the mosquito. She was really glad that sucker was dead.

"Where are you?"

"I'm out in the woods. I'm one of them that escaped."

"Where are you calling from?"

She ignored the question and gave them the directions Henry had given her.

"Your voice sounds different now."

"I just got over a cold."

"Just now?"

"I think so. Yes. It just left me. I took some medicine."

There was a period of silence on the dispatcher's end of the phone, and then, "There are a lot of oak trees."

"What?"

"Directions you gave you said there was an oak tree."

"Oh. Well, this one is big and some limbs have been cut off."

"What's as far as you can holler?"

"You can figure it out. I got to go. I got something on the stove."

Jane hung up.

When Jane came back to sit by Henry, Henry said, "You get it explained?"

"Maybe."

"You disguised your voice."

"I finally figured since they don't know my voice, wasn't any reason to disguise it."

"Oh, yeah. I hadn't thought of that."

THEY got up and looked around and found a tool shed out back of the liquor store. It was unlocked. They slid open the door and looked inside. There wasn't anything in it but a shovel. They stretched out on the floor and slept.

Jane worried all night that the police would trace her call to the phone booth, but by late morning the cops had still not arrived. She got up and found that Henry was gone.

She walked around to the front of the liquor store. Through the glass she saw Henry inside. She was sitting in a chair that was pulled up to the counter, and there was a different man behind the counter than last night. He was younger, had a wispy beard and unruly hair, and was so thin it looked as if his shirt were hanging on a coat hanger instead of shoulders. They had paper cups in front of them and Henry picked hers up and sipped from it.

Jane came inside.

"I was just telling Clifton here how we are two travelers of the road. Except for last night. He doesn't care we slept in the shed out back. He doesn't mind I smell like cow shit."

"Not my shed," Clifton said. "I grew up around cows, so I'm okay with the smell. You want some coffee?"

"Oh, heavens yes," Jane said.

Clifton brought a chair out from behind the counter and placed it next to Henry and the counter. "I'll get you some coffee. You like sugar in it, and some of that powdered milk stuff?"

"I'll take it all, and thanks."

"Ah, no problem. It's just coffee. Someone comes in, you'll have to move while they pay up. This time of morning we just get a wino or two mostly."

Jane sat in the chair. After a night of sleeping on the hard floor, it felt good to sit. Her neck was stiff, though. Up close she saw that Clifton had once had a bad case of acne, and it had pocked his face like a pumice stone.

"I got some doughnuts back here," Clifton said. "I bought them this morning. They're a mixture. I got sugar powdered ones, some with jam or chocolate or some such in them. I just bought a bunch. I like to nibble on them all day. I can't gain a pound, though I'd like to. Doughnuts might as well be water to me."

"They stick to my ass," Jane said, "but I'll have one, with jam in it if that's all right."

"Those are the good ones all right," Henry said. "I've already had one. Dip it in the coffee."

A moment later Clifton placed a partially empty box of doughnuts on the counter then went away and fixed the coffee the way Jane liked it. He brought it back. She hovered over the doughnut box for a moment, like a hawk choosing a mouse, stuck to her plan and picked up one of the jam-filled doughnuts. The red jam was seeping out of little holes in the doughnut, and Jane took a big bite. The jam exploded in her mouth and it was a tasteful explosion. Strawberry. Followed by the coffee, it was pretty divine.

"I been on the road myself," Clifton said. "It's nice someone is nice to you. You can make the trip if you can find enough nice folks. Have folks been nice to you?"

"It's a bit more complicated than that," Henry said. "But you have certainly been nice."

"I like your eye patch," Clifton said.

"Why thank you. It's a new addition to my fashion ensemble."

"I went on the road because of Jack Kerouac," Clifton said, leaning forward and placing his elbows on the counter and supporting his chin with his hands.

"Who?" Henry said.

"He was a writer back in the fifties that wrote about taking a road trip with a friend. He went everywhere and had all kinds of adventures. He typed his novel on a big roll of paper and wrote it quick and didn't use as much punctuation as you might, and he had a lot of on purpose run-on sentences."

"I always got a C– on account of run on sentences," Henry said.

"It's called artistic license," Jane said.

"There you go," Clifton said. "I was going to do like he done. You know, write out all I had done. But I pretty much just rode in cars with folks who talked about stuff I can't remember. I got out to San Francisco, though. I got my momma to send me some money to take a plane back."

"Did you write about it?"

"I thought about it, but like I said, I couldn't remember anything I had talked about with anyone, except an old boy who liked to go fishing. We talked about bass mostly. Like to fish, you can talk about bass a long time, though conversations about perch don't last too long. I tried to write it all down, but that writing stuff is hard. There was this old boy that had written some stories and novels, and I went to him and told him I had this story, but couldn't write it down. He said 'that's the trick, isn't it?' Just like that. That, ladies, was a revelation for me. I asked him to write it down for me, make up stuff, and when it got published we could split the money. He said 'I got stories of my own. I don't need yours.' I thought that was rude, but that too was a revelation."

"What would you say the revelations were?" Jane said.

"That I didn't have a story to tell and I can't write, and no one else wants to write for me. Simple really. But profound too. I learned right then I didn't really like being on the road and I ought to get a regular job, and here I am. I'm learning the guitar in my free time. I think maybe I could be in a band, though I'd just have to play, because I can't sing."

"How are the guitar lessons going?" Henry asked, fishing out another doughnut from the box. Jane noted it was one with powdered sugar on it.

"I teach myself, actually. I got a book and this DVD. It's pretty hard though. I get a note down, and then I wake up the next morning, it's like I never learned it. Lot of stuff I like is played in E, so I'm trying to learn the ins and outs of E."

The door opened and a woman came in. She had a big hairdo and it was thick and red. You could see she had green eyes even from a distance. They were like emeralds. She was wearing a short bluejean dress and a white shirt with blue butterflies on it and she wore it with a bluejean vest. She had on black cowboy boots with red toe explosions and the boots had higher heels than normal. She was maybe five seven and built well, like she had been designed by the gods.

She rolled nicely when she walked.

"Goddamn," she said. "Didn't think I'd ever find a liquor store. I drove all night from Ft. Worth, and once I got outside of there, well, I couldn't find anything but beer, and I wanted whisky."

She stopped at the counter.

"Howdy, ladies. That's my stage talk. Howdy."

"What stage?" Henry said.

"Any stage. I travel all over playing music. I had a couple hits once, and what they got me was that red Cadillac convertible outside, some nice clothes and a bit of money that's long spent and a bad case of the clap once. That's cured up though, in case you're curious. I got to stay steady on the road just to pay for the hotels and such. It's not much of a life, but music is my life. For now. I'm thinking of taking up real estate in a couple of years if things don't get better."

Jane thought this was a lot of information.

"You aren't drinking and driving, are you?" Jane said.

"Nope, but I want some whisky for when I hole up somewhere. I plan to get so drunk if winos see me they'd be embarrassed."

Clifton hadn't moved since the woman came in. His mouth was slightly open and there was spittle in the corners of it.

"You might want to shut that mouth, Liquor Man, before a fly gets in it."

"You're Cheryle Banker, aren't you?"

"All day every day all day long," Cheryle said. "What I'd like is a bottle of Wild Turkey, and something meaner if you got it. Price could be a deal breaker, though, so don't bag it till we tag it."

"Yes, ma'am," Clifton said, and went on a whisky hunt.

"What are you ladies doing hanging out in a liquor store drinking coffee. Oh, hell, doughnuts. Do you mind?"

"Not ours," Jane said.

"Better yet." Cheryle nabbed one and took a big bite. "Oh god, I live on lettuce and tomatoes most of the time, and not even full-grown tomatoes, but them little bitty ones and a radish now and then to keep my ass in this dress as well as the others I got damn near like it. But now and then, I got to caution the seams in my outfits a bit. I like that eye patch, girl. You wear it for looks or you got a fucked-up eye."

"Fucked-up eye," Henry said.

"Well, either way, it looks good on you. I had to wear a patch when I was little. Lazy eye. I wore glasses over it. It didn't look good on me, but you're rocking it, lady."

"Thanks," Henry said.

"You girls been rolling in cow shit?"

"Not exactly," Jane said, "but we are coated in essence of cow's ass."

Clifton came back with the whisky. He put two bottles on the counter said, "I got all your albums."

"That means you got two. I had a couple hits, then I didn't, and the goddamn label dropped me. I fucked everyone in Nashville for a new contract after that. But it didn't help. I made an album myself. I was going to show them. Used my own money. I tried to sell them on Amazon, but I got about twelve sales a month and some good reviews from relatives. Now I got about four boxes of them CDs in the trunk of my Cadillac. I sell them at shows, but even people who like your music would rather steal it off the internet. They're pretty sure it's their privilege. Well, how much do I owe you?"

Clifton said, "You got that CD you done yourself in your car trunk, I'll damn sure buy one of them. That's one I don't have."

"You and most people. But sure."

"You'll sign it?"

"All over the place. Let me go out and get it."

Cheryle put down money for the whisky and went outside to get the CD. She walked away as briskly as she had come in.

"Damn," Henry said. "I feel like I been through a whirlwind."

"I like her music so much," Clifton said.

"I think you like more than her music," Henry said.

"Who wouldn't?" Clifton said.

"You look like you're about to wet yourself, though."

"I already did. A little. I'm just kidding."

"I hope so."

Cheryle came back in with the CD. She put it on the counter. It was a photo of her wearing the same outfit, except the shirt was blue and the butterflies were white.

"I got this look people expect. I really prefer house shoes and stretchy pants, but you got to play the star, you know."

"You play it well," Clifton said.

"I know, but that don't necessarily make you one. You girls, you just come here and sit around in a liquor store all day, eat doughnuts and smell like cow shit?"

"We're on the road," Jane said. "Trying to get up north. She's going to Boston, and I'm going a little farther."

"You girls are in luck, if you can put up with two stops and two shows I got before Boston, where I got three pretty good gigs, you can ride with me."

Jane calculated the time she needed to get to the wedding. She had some time to spare, but this could be the ticket.

"Just to let you know, if you cause me any trouble, I will whip your ass and shoot you. I got a gun permit and a little pistol to go with it. Girl on the road has got to be careful. Thing is, I don't even like guns, but now everyone else has one or two, so I didn't want to be left out."

"You won't have to shoot us," Henry said.

"That's good. Because I lied. I have neither permit or gun. I loathe them, but I can bluff the shit out of a wild hog if it comes to it. But you two, I trust. Besides, I think I can whip at least one of you in an unfair fight and make it not worth the other's effort."

"No problem from us," Jane said.

Cheryle pulled a Sharpie from her inside vest pocket and smiled big at Clifton, and then prepared to signed the CD.

Clifton said, "Can you say, 'To Clifton?'"

"How about, 'With all my sweet love to Clifton?' No one has to think it's really love, but they might think we're fucking."

"Oh, hell yeah," Clifton said.

NINETEEN

THE convertible was bright red and it shimmered in the sunlight and the top was down.

"One in the front, and one in the back, choose your spots. Trunk's full of my stuff, so you'll have to ride your luggage on the back seat."

They put their meager luggage on the driver's side of the back seat, and then Jane climbed in the front passenger side, and Henry sat behind her in the back seat.

As Cheryle slipped in behind the wheel, she said, "You gals look like you've had a hard road."

"Oh, nothing really," Jane said.

"Y'all just mess around in cow shit as a matter of course?"

"Just being on the road trying to get north," Jane said, "and we've had problems with a car, and the bus didn't go where we need to go."

"Well, y'all sit back and rest, nap if you like. I'm going to drive until I need to pee."

Jane closed her eyes and felt the wind blowing her hair. It was a cool wind on a bright day, and before she knew it, she was sound asleep.

THEY drove all day and finally when night came, they pulled into a Walmart parking lot. It was the same trick Jane and Henry had tried at Save-Mart, but Jane didn't bring up their misadventure there.

After Cheryle put up the convertible's roof, they all went inside to take advantage of the restroom and buy McDonald's burgers which were in the back of the store, then they went out to the car again. They climbed in and ate their burgers and drank their sodas.

"I want you to know this is where we're bedding down tonight," Cheryle said. "I could probably buy a hotel room for the night, well, a motel, some cheap-ass place, but I'm saving my money for a yacht."

"Won't that take a lot of time to save?" Jane asked.

"She's pulling your leg, Jane," Henry said.

"Yeah," Cheryle said. "I'm more likely to get a row boat and a bass rig, some fishing worms on credit."

"Do you get tired being on the road?" Jane asked.

"I have been tired of it for some time, but as my other choices are prostitution or being a waitress, I stay at it, though I have considered prostitution, as I already know my way around a motel room."

"Are you going to record again?" Jane asked.

"Costs money to record, and I've burned all my bridges in Nashville. I was thinking about going out to Hollywood and trying to be an actress. I figure I can fail at that about as easy as I can music."

"But you had some hits," Henry said.

"Yeah, and those have sustained me. They were popular enough I can play at dives and bars, and a lot of the time the only thing the men in the audience, because it's mostly men, are interested in is looking up my dress. But what hurts is when that doesn't even interest them. They just want to talk over the music and yell to their buddies about all the women they're banging and the biggest deer they shot."

"You don't have a band?" Henry asked.

"Sometimes I hire people I know where I'm playing. Lot of good players out there, but these days I mostly just play guitar myself and sing. I'm nothing special on the guitar, but I get by. I play and hope I get paid. That's sometimes a problem. I don't do percentage of the house deals anymore. I have a set fee, but a lot of times it turns out I have it set, but the owners of the shitholes where I play have a more flexible viewpoint. Kind of pay if they want. I tell you true, I think this is my last trip on the road. I'm thirty-four and I've had enough of this shit. What I need to find is a rich husband pushing ninety with a good insurance policy and a bad heart."

"I guess it all just seems glamorous," Jane said.

"There's glamour for some, but for me, not so much. I had my window, but I didn't get through it in time. Well, I had some success, but I spent too much time on bad men and bad investments. Let me tell you, the all-purpose garden hose I invested money in wasn't that all-purpose. It was just a goddamn water hose. My manager talked me into that. He ended up with my money and I got a couple of water hoses out of the deal. They were flexible all right, and you could stand them straight up and they'd spew water. Looked like a big ole snake on your lawn spitting all over the place. Turned out though, they already had something called sprinklers that did the job and didn't look creepy and were way cheaper to buy. I didn't think that one through. They were going to have ads on TV and all over, but that didn't happen. They did a newspaper ad or two about it, and turned out there wasn't a factory where they made that shit. Just had a few examples, which is what I got out of the lawsuit. Lawyer made out all right. My manager, shit, he went to Costa Rica. I don't think anyone's looking for him or my investment. By now I bet he's done spent it on women and whisky and song and Batman action figures. He collected them. Well, enough about me, you can read my autobiography when it comes out. I'm ready to sleep, and that's something I'm an expert at. I can snooze on a bed of tacks if I have to."

Cheryle leaned her seat back. Jane did the same. Henry stretched out on the back seat. Pretty soon, they were all asleep.

WHEN Jane awoke it was morning and the sun was bright through the windshield. Except for Henry's snoring, it seemed like a wonderful morning. She wasn't sure why she felt so good, but she decided it was a good night's sleep. She hadn't even thought about what had happened out at the compound. She hoped Ilene had made it home. She hoped all the escaped women had found a place to go. She wondered if the police had followed her directions and if they could figure out how far a holler was.

When she looked to where Cheryle was sleeping, she discovered she was gone. She used the lever on her seat to sit it upright, and no sooner than she did, Cheryle appeared at the door and got in with her purse slung over her shoulder, carrying a plastic bag. She sat the bag between them and took out a bottle of cold coffee. She looked as crisp and beautiful as when they first saw her. Jane figured she had washed up a bit in the bathroom, though she was wearing the same clothes.

"I didn't think I could balance the hot ones and carry three, even in a cardboard tray, so I bought these."

"Fine by me," Jane said.

"And I got a small box of doughnuts. Yesterday I done bad eating one that what's his name offered—"

"Clifton," Jane said.

"Yeah, him. But damn, I'm on a roll now."

Henry, alerted by their conversation, sat up in the back seat. "I slept like a stone," she said.

"And snored like a lawn mower," Jane said.

"Sorry," Henry said.

"I didn't even hear it," Cheryle said.

"It didn't keep me from sleeping," Jane said, "but you were sure mowing grass when I woke up."

Cheryle offered Henry a bottle of cold coffee, and she was delighted to have it. They ate a couple doughnuts apiece. When they were done, Jane took off her shoe and fished out ten dollars and gave it to Cheryle. "For gas money."

"I ought to be real hesitant about taking it, you know, waiting until the third offer to accept it, but we can use some gas and I'm afraid you might just offer it once, so thank you."

Cheryle took the money and carefully removed a small change purse from her larger purse and put the ten in it.

By mid-morning they had finished breakfast, lowered the convertible top, got gas, and were wheeling on down the highway, exceeding the speed limit by fifteen to twenty miles an hour, and sometimes more. Cheryle had a heavy foot.

Cheryle was on her cell phone yelling above the sound of the wind roaring by, flicking her red hair about so savagely it looked as it were a raging fire. Somehow, none of it ever whipped into her mouth, contrary to Jane's situation, where she was constantly spitting out or pulling her hair from between her teeth.

Cheryle was having a fairly heated discussion with someone on the other end of her call. Jane wished she had a cell phone. She needed to get one. She needed to get her teeth cleaned and a good hot bath right then wouldn't have hurt either. She felt coated in day old sweat and grit and cow shit.

"Well, that's one less gig," Cheryle said when she finished her call. "That little motherfucker only wanted to pay me half of what he promised on account of he said he had half the crowd last time I was there, half of what I used to bring in to his place. I guess those hits of mine are getting old, but I tell you, I work for half of what I'm getting now, I'm not making enough money to go through the problem of straining my voice. My voice is my instrument, and sometimes it can go haywire when it's used too much. And they still smoke in that place. It's outside the city limits. You leave there, you smell like you been in a tobacco barn fire, so I'm just as glad to mark it off my list."

"Sorry," Jane said.

"No sweat. Crowd at that place is the worst. They are always yelling at you to take off your top or pull your dress up over your thigh. They think you're up there to strip, way they act. I didn't get into music for that. Far as I'm concerned that club and its owner can suck shit through a straw and call it malted milk."

Jane glanced back at Henry. She was leaned back in the seat with her eyes closed and the wind was working her short hair. The sun was on her face. Jane thought if Henry stayed that way long, she'd have to disturb her on account of she'd get sunburned, but then it occurred to her with the top down, no matter which way you sat, unless it was with a bag over your head, the sun shining on you was a certainty.

They drove along for a few hours and stopped only momentarily at a hamburger place to go in and use the restroom and wash up a bit and change clothes. Jane discovered that after changing her clothes, and the wash down, she smelled all right and she felt better in clean clothes, even if they were as wrinkled as an octogenarian's throat. She stuffed her cow shit duds in a tall trash can, deciding it was better than mixing them in with her other clean items. After they had all spruced up a bit, they bought burgers and sat in the back of the joint and ate them.

Back in the car, by late afternoon, it was starting to look like rain. Cheryle pulled over and put the top up and drove on. The rain clouds darkened and then there were a few drops, and finally the rain was heavy and the windshield wipers slapped at it until the rain finally broke. By then the sun was going down and they were driving into South Carolina.

"I don't want to say people here are backwards, as they're among the people who buy my music, but once I saw a wedding dress in a children's store."

"Damn," Henry said.

"Yeah. It was on sale."

"Damn," Henry said again.

When they got to North Carolina, it was solid dark and they were soon off the highway and cruising through a little town that was mostly closed up, except for a fast food restaurant with a few cars parked at it.

Cheryle guided the car down a long dark road and finally they came to a well-lit building out in the sticks. There was a sign on it that said, BOBBY JOE'S ROADHOUSE.

"This place is a notch up from the one I told you about earlier, which means most of the men here remember to zip up their flys," Cheryle said. "You can come in or stay in the car. Here's the plus. I can get you two in free of charge. Here's the downside, you'll be inside."

"I'll chance it," Jane said. "I'd like to hear you sing."

"I'm in too," Henry said.

They got out of the car and Cheryle got her guitar case from the trunk and lugged it to the back door of the place, and went inside. It smelled like beer and sweat and wet dog fur in there. Jane didn't see a wet dog, though.

There was a door open in the hallway and light was coming out of it. Cheryle led them in there. It was a small room and the open door had a small white sign with the word OFFICE on it in bold black letters. There was a man sitting behind his desk with his feet up. He had on a cowboy hat and a green and white cowboy shirt with snap buttons on it, and he was wearing jeans. He had a long face and a broad chin and looked quite proud of himself. There was a wad of what might have been dog shit on the heel of one of his boots. He was reading a comic book. He put the book on the desk top.

"I was thinking you might not show," the man said. "Who are these people?"

"This is Jane and Henry. They're traveling with me."

"Henry, that's a funny name for a girl."

"I don't know," Henry said. "I don't laugh about it much."

"This here is Travis Hamm," Cheryle said. "He owns this shithole. He leads Baptist Bible study on Sundays."

"Thanks for that introduction, Cheryle. And being a shithole, we can't always afford the best entertainment, so you'll have to do, darling."

"I can't dispute that," Cheryle said.

"You got dog shit on your boot heel," Henry said.

"What's that?"

Henry pointed.

He pulled his feet off the desk and put the foot Henry had pointed at across his knee, bent over and looked at the boot heel. "Well, hell. I got so many dogs at home I could use a dog sled to get to work."

"You'd need snow," Henry said.

"You're a practical one, aren't you? How'd you lose your eye?"

"Hawk clawed it out."

"I doubt that."

"Snake bite."

"Now that's getting rich."

"All right, if you two are through playing, I'd like to get this on the road," Cheryle said. "Two hours performance, half of the money now."

"I'm good for it," Travis said. He had pulled a trash can over and was using a pencil to scrape the dog shit off his boot heel and into the can.

"You'll be better for it if you pay me half now, like always."

"I could just turn on the jukebox."

"You could," Cheryle said, "and I'll give you a quarter to play a tune, one of mine if it's on there."

"It isn't."

"Then most any tune will do, and after we all pat our feet and nod our heads to the music, me and my friends will load up and leave."

"I ain't making much money, Cheryle. Live music ain't like it used to be. Everyone downloads for free and they like canned music at a joint much as live music. Better. Everything you hear has been a hit and it's easier to talk over."

"But you're a patron of the arts, Travis. Pay me half. Now."

"Damn, Cheryle. You're kind of a bully."

"No, I'm kind of experienced."

Travis finished scraping his boot heel and pulled a Kleenex from a box on his desk and used it to wipe up the heel. He took his time doing it, then put the Kleenex in the trash. He then wrestled a key from his tight pants pocket without standing up, and used it to open a desk drawer. He pulled out a small metal box. He used another key from his pocket to open the box. Inside the box was another key. He took that key and went to the back wall, slid some wood paneling aside, and in the wall was a safe that you could open with a key.

He used the key, and inside the safe was another metal box. It was silver and shiny. The same key opened that one. He stood with his back to them as he rooted around in the box and came out with a clutch of bills. He shoved those in his pants pocket, making a wad about the size of a small groundhog.

He put the box back inside and went through the process in reverse. Then, facing them again, he pulled the bills out of his pocket and put them on the desk near Cheryle.

Cheryle put her guitar case on the floor, picked up the money, counted it "Really, Travis? Half of it in ones?"

"Wednesday night we run a stripper pole. Our most popular night. They give the girls tips in ones, and we have a rule that we get half of that."

"That's cheap, Travis," Cheryle said.

"What can I say. I'm cheap. Ever need to earn extra money, Cheryle, my dear, I can set you up if you got your own G-string."

"All right, goddamn it, let's get this party started," Cheryle said, after giving Travis a look that could have knocked a hawk off a barbwire fence at thirty paces.

Picking up her guitar case, she took a deep breath and they all left the room, except Travis. Jane and Henry followed Cheryle down the dog-smelling hall and through another door, into a room lit mostly by neon signs that advertised beer. There was a bar at the far end, and most of the signs were there on the wall above the bar. There was a mirror and there were lots of bottles, and one of the neon signs blinked blue and red lights, and the light from it made the bottles light up like something magical was inside of them; some might say that indeed there was. At least until morning came when they puked the magic out.

The air was thick with smoke, both cigarettes and marijuana, belying the once upon a time sacred country boy verses of Merle Haggard's famous song "Okie from Muskogee." Of course, there was the bite of alcohol in the air as well, and the kind of smell all bars have that's undefinable. Jane thought of it as the stench of hopeful regret, whatever that was, but it's what came to mind anytime she entered a bar. Before tonight, her last entry had ended up with her in a preacher's car and then running naked through a ditch out back of a church. She decided she might have a diet cola and some bar peanuts.

Jane looked around and saw that there were indeed peanuts on the bar, but she hesitated. She checked the crowd. It was nearly all men, but a few women were identifiable in the shadows, silent as gnus drinking from a crocodile-infested waterhole.

Cheryle didn't so much as stop to get her bearings. She walked up on the dark stage, opened her guitar case and plugged into the already on-stage equipment. She stood in front of the microphone and turned it on, tapped her fingers against it. When she did the microphone gave out with little thumps. Cheryle immediately started tuning her guitar.

Jane and Henry blended into the shadows near the stage and found a place on the wall to lean. Jane eyed the bar from there, and the bowl of peanuts. She saw a large jar at the far end of the bar and thought that it might contain pickled pigs feet. Not a favorite, but right then she was so hungry she was considering cannibalism. In fact, she had her eye on a plump cowboy who was sitting in the back against the wall with his hat pulled down to cover his face. He might have been asleep, or had died in the dark.

By this time, Cheryle had been noted by the crowd, and the wolf whistles started, along with compliments on her attire and shape. Just the sort of thing drunk rednecks think women love to hear, or at least what they figure their comrades enjoyed hearing. A sacred right of manhood; assholism and measuring their dicks.

"Hey baby," one man was yelling. "Let me tune you up. Turn on the lights so we can get a good look."

Cheryle hadn't so much as turned her attention away from her guitar, but feeling now she had tuned it enough, she put her mouth close to the microphone and said, "Mike check. Mike check."

"Hey," said the shouting man. "My name is Mike. Come over here and check me over."

Cheryle shot him the finger, and the man laughed as if she had given him her hotel key. He went back to shouting what he thought was enticing love talk, and then a man about the size of a mountain with snow on top, the snow being a white cowboy hat, rose from a chair and walked over to the shouter, and punched him out of his chair. He lay silent on the floor.

"Why thank you," Cheryle said into the microphone.

"Welcome," the big man said.

A few more moments passed while Cheryle attempted to adjust the knobs on the ancient stage equipment. Either satisfied or defeated at her attempt to adjust the knobs, she walked back to the microphone, said, "Well, this equipment is as shitty as last time I was here, but I'm Cheryle, and here we go."

She broke into a number that was more rock than country, and it was a good one. The equipment may have been old, but it seemed to be working fine that night. The licks on her guitar were not fancy, but they were sharp and clear as spring water. Her voice was a fine contrast, growling and barking, and then going smooth, rising up, and dropping down. She had complete control.

Jane realized she had heard the song, and she knew then this was one of the hits Cheryle had been living on. Before she realized it, she was tapping her foot and swaying a little. Henry might as well have been a stone statue. She had the demeanor of someone just trying to get through it all.

After a bit, the few women who were there with husbands or dates got up and started to dance. Cheryle finished up the rocker, and rocked another one. She knew that a crowd wanted something rowdy on the weekend, not love ballads. They wanted to sweat out their ho-hum lives, and for the moment move about inside some sort of dark and smoky dream, enhanced by adult beverages.

The big man with the big white hat got up and walked over toward where Jane and Henry leaned against the wall. He walked directly to Jane, said, "Would you care to dance, little lady?"

It was pretty cliché, but Jane found it worked, and she held out her hand and he took it. She glanced back at Henry. A grin moved in one corner of Henry's mouth, then went into hiding.

Out on the dance floor the big man showed he had some moves. They were actually rock dancing, as Jane thought of it. Not touching one another, just being close and getting their groove on. She could see the man a little better out there where the neon was brighter from the bar. He wasn't bad looking, not at all, and he was big enough to hold the Statue of Liberty's torch while she powdered her nose.

He leaned in and told her his name was Charlie, and she told him her name, and then Cheryle played and sang a slower one, and they held each other and swayed. She hoped she didn't smell too aromatic from her days on the road.

Most of Cheryle's song list was loud and rocking, and she was really good, or so Jane thought, but then again, she didn't run a record label.

Time flew by, and pretty soon it was time for Cheryle to take a break, and by then Jane realized again that she was really hungry, and she asked if they might go to the bar and get a drink and clutch at peanuts, maybe a pigs foot.

Charlie was buying. He couldn't believe she wanted a diet drink, but he bought it for her, along with a beer for himself, and they sat on stools at the bar and drank and ate peanuts from a bowl. Jane tried not to gobble. She noted the pig feet again, but decided they looked as if they might have been there since the first hog walked the earth. The pickle juice looked a little rusty with parts of meat floating around in it, and the bottom of the jar had a sludgy buildup reminiscent of the contents of a foot bath.

Charlie explained how he was quite the cattleman, and bragged on his ranch, which he said was in the mountains. All of it sounded like bar bullshit, but Jane went along with it. She told him she was a successful real estate lady on holiday with her good friends Cheryle and Henry, and thanked him for standing up for Cheryle, and she added that he had a good punch and was quick for a big man.

He said, "Ah, that's all right. You don't talk to a lady like he did."

Charlie said he had all of Cheryle's records, except for one she did of folk tunes. He couldn't stand folk tunes since he had been forced to sing "If I Had a Hammer" in a third-grade school play. He felt he could have done better with something more contemporary.

Jane was uncertain which of Cheryle's three CDs that was. She might bother to ask later, and she might not.

In the closer neon light, Jane could see Charlie was older than she had first thought. Still handsome, but it had been maybe fifty years since he sang "If I Had a Hammer" in third grade. Still he was pleasant enough and a lot less sullen to talk to than Henry.

Thinking on this, she looked around for Henry, who had abandoned her place on the wall. Finally, she saw her at one of the tables sitting with a man with slicked back black hair. They were arm wrestling.

Charlie noting what Jane was seeing, said, "Ain't that your one-eyed friend?"

"Well, there's not two of her, I'll tell you that. She's one of a kind."

Henry slammed the man's hand down on the table, then held out her hand, palm up. The man picked up some bills he had placed on the table and gave them to her. Henry was making some travel money.

Cheryle came back from break and slipped herself back into the guitar strap. She started with a kind of medium sounding song that gained momentum like a carefully orchestrated sex act, and then she really began to rock, playing guitar better than in other songs. She was thumping it with her fingers too, giving it a kind of beat.

"I don't think we ought to miss this one," Charlie said, and they went out on the dance floor.

As the night wore on, Charlie drank beer after beer and professed undying love and offered Jane a place in his home, if she didn't mind his kids at Christmas, all grown now, and their divorced mama tucked away in a nut house in Charleston.

Jane actually thought about it a few seconds, but she just smiled, and Charlie talked on with all the things they could do together until his voice wore out. After he ordered "One more beer," a mantra he had repeated after each beer, and another diet soda for Jane, he fell asleep sitting in a chair with his hand wrapped around a beer bottle, the music pounding the bar hard enough chairs were rattling. This wasn't a disturbance to Charlie. A buffalo herd could have run through and the only way he might have noticed was if they knocked his chair over.

For comparison she checked the fat man with his hat down that had been sleeping against the wall. Nope, that guy was the leader. He hadn't so much as lifted his head or patted a foot. If he was in fact dead, however, that might disqualify him.

Jane patted Charlie's large hand. "You were sweet."

She got up as Cheryle said goodnight, unplugged her guitar and put it in the guitar case. Cheryle was already walking toward the back, and Henry had appeared from nowhere and was following after. Jane gave Charlie one more look, imagined her at home with him, helping him adjust his false teeth in a few years and changing his bed pans. She went after Henry and Cheryle.

In the hallway the shadowed dream of the bar gave way to cheap wallpaper and squeaking floor boards.

Cheryle stopped at Travis's office door, tried to turn the knob. It was locked.

"Damn it," Cheryle said, placed the guitar case on the floor near the wall and took out a pistol from one of the case's inside pockets.

"I thought you said you didn't have a gun," Jane said.

"I lied. It's the permit I don't have."

Cheryle backed away from the door, hiked up her dress, and gave the door her boot. It creaked. She kicked again and the lock gave way with a snap and she was inside the office as fast as a cop at a drug bust.

Travis was sitting behind his desk.

"Now there wasn't any call for that, Cheryle," he said. "You didn't knock."

"I knocked last year, and we know how long that took."

Travis looked to Jane and Henry for sympathy. "She does this every year, comes in here with a gun. What kind of reputation do you think that gives her? She lacks patience. That's the word on her. No patience."

"Just give me my money, Travis," Cheryle said. "And don't expect me back next year."

"You weren't going to be invited. Hell, we're getting the place fixed up with sound that will go all through the bar, and after the payout for that, we don't have to mess with ill-tempered, bullying performers with pistols."

"The money," Cheryle said.

"Will you take a check?"

"No."

Travis went through the ritual of before, finally opening the money box and sorting out some bills, as if he were rationing food to a starving army.

"Just give me what you owe me," Cheryle said.

Finally, Travis laid the money on the table.

"Would you pick that up, Henry, if you please? I want to be ready to shoot him between the eyes if he tries to disarm me."

"I ain't gonna try and disarm you. And I bet you'll be looking to come back next year, and I won't need you."

"Don't hold your breath," Cheryle said.

Henry picked up the money and she and Jane backed out of the open door and into the hallway.

"'Course," Travis said, "we still got that Fourth of July picnic thing. We'll need you for that."

"I'll think on it," Cheryle said.

When they were out at the car the night had cleared of clouds and the moon and starlight were bright.

"Oh, Jesus," Jane said. "I thought you might really shoot him."

"With a cap gun? Nope. It looks real, don't it?"

She gave the gun to Jane who looked at it and laughed. "It does."

"We do that about every year, but him putting in sound to replace singers, I believe that. He's cheap. Hell, he probably knows the gun is a cap gun. He's as dramatic as I am. I'll most likely do the picnic, by the way. He arranges it, but the people who pay me are a lot less trouble and they provide a real good spread."

TWENTY

CHERYLE drove through the night. Somewhere between North Carolina and Virginia, Jane fell asleep. She dreamed this time, and the dream was of General Mumu, looking up at her through the back windshield of the car Henry stole. Her eyes were big and her face was scrunched and Wispy's hair was floating up in front of her, and then the whole car was filled with water. In the dream, General Mumu turned into a fat mermaid and tried to swim out of the window but was too big for it. She was struggling for an exit when Jane awoke.

It was daylight. The convertible top was down and the wind was cool and the pace was swift.

Jane looked over at Cheryle. "Damn, girl, I'm sorry. I can drive some."

"Nah, that's all right. I'm a driving bitch. I like to drive. I can go nearly two days without sleep. Not saying that's how I like to live on a regular basis, not sleeping for two days, I mean, but when I'm on the road, I believe in putting the pedal to the metal. First time in a while I haven't gotten a speeding ticket."

They stopped for one more gig, and this one was at a pizza parlor in West Virginia. Cheryle played for a hundred dollars and tips. There was a stage and there were some mechanical bears on either side of her and they danced a robotic dance that never changed in pacing, no matter the nature of the music. Jane thought they danced better than a Boy Band.

When Cheryle wrapped up her time, got her pay and carried off her tips in her guitar case, Jane and Henry helped her carry two free boxes of cheese pizza and three sodas.

Cheryle said as they stepped out into the night and crossed the parking lot, "I probably made less than the waitresses."

"But you got to be up in front of people," Jane said. "Those waitresses weren't singing. Lots of people can wait tables, but not everyone can sing."

"That's true."

"And no one pinched you on the ass," Henry said.

"Also true."

Cheryle put the guitar case in the trunk of the car and then they sat in the convertible and ate pizza and drank sodas.

"I'm definitely going to have to let this dress out after this week," Cheryle said. She popped open her phone and checked GPS coordinates, then closed it. "All right, we are some traveling bitches. Let's say it. Which way are we going?"

"North," Henry said.

"Which way?"

"North," they all said.

Jane stood up on the floorboard, took a dramatic stance, and pointed over the windshield, up toward the North Star. Or what she thought was the North Star, and said simply, "North."

THE night before they arrived in Boston they stopped at a little motel and paid for two beds. Henry and Jane slept in one, Cheryle, who put in the bulk of the room money, got a bed all her own.

Jane mentally prepared for tomorrow. She would catch one of those buses she hated out of Boston and arrive where she needed to be within a few hours of the wedding.

They were all sitting up in their beds with the light out, and Jane was telling Henry and Cheryle about the wedding plans.

"They're having the reception across the street at Big Bob's Steak House. There was a note inside the invitation that explained it all."

"I know that place," Cheryle said. "I know where you'll be. I played there a few times, at the steakhouse, not the motel. They have half-price steaks on Tuesdays."

"Yeah, well, I'll be there tomorrow, and that's Wednesday. A half-price steak would have been good."

"They'll have some kind of wedding dinner laid out, so you'll be fine. And you'll get there in plenty of time tomorrow. I mapped out the trip on my phone to the bus station. You get to where you're going, bus station ain't but a block away from the motel and the steakhouse. You'll get there in plenty of time to get all froo-frooed up."

"Bet I'm the only one arriving by bus," Jane said.

"Don't matter if you come on the back of a buzzard if you get there in time. Damn, I'm going to miss you two. Henry, I been meaning to ask. Other night, arm wrestling, did you lose any?"

"One, but he had an arm like a tree falling on you, but the rest I won. I lost two dollars to the tree arm, but I gained twenty-five overall. I always had strong arms and I lift weights. Also, I know how to cheat a little with positioning and all."

"I was curious. I almost quit singing once during a tense match. I had to quit watching, I was getting so involved."

Jane went into the bathroom, and after she was showered and washed her hair and dried it, she opened her suitcase and looked at her little black dress. As she pulled it out, she saw that the light shone through it in a large spot at the rear. A terrible realization came over her. She had owned the dress so long her butt had worn it thin and shiny at the rear. She couldn't wear it anymore. She was devastated.

She put on her sleeping clothes, underwear and a long T-shirt and came out of the bathroom carrying her suitcase.

"You look like someone ran over your dog," Cheryle said.

"It's the dress I was going to wear. It's grown kind of thin in the butt. I hadn't noticed until now."

"Too thin to wear?" Henry said.

"I'm afraid so. The right light they can see what digested food group is coming down the pike. Buying one is out of my budget, and I still need to buy a wedding present."

"Well," Cheryle said. "I might not have the most appropriate dress for a wedding, but I got a dress you might can wear."

Cheryle opened up her suitcase and pulled out one of the outfits she wore on stage. It was bright red with blue rhinestones and had Country and Western V-shaped pocket flaps on it. "I can't say it's the right dress, but it is a dress."

Jane studied it. Her options were few.

"I also got an extra pair of boots to go with it. I'm thinking I'm not going to need them after this run. I'm all wore out being on the road. It's time to find that old man I told you about, one with lots of money and the Grim Reaper following him around."

Jane took the dress into the bathroom and tried it on. She came out and showed it to them.

"Hell," Henry said. "You look fine."

"You do," Cheryle said. "You got the shape for that. It always cut off my circulation."

"It's kind of short. High on the thighs."

"You got the legs for it," Cheryle said.

Jane tried the boots on. They were bright blue with shiny yellow stars on the toes. They fit.

"Guess this is it," Jane said.

"When they pronounce them man and wife, you yell, 'Yeehaw,'" Cheryle said.

AS they were driving to the bus station the next day, Jane saw a sign for Save-Mart.

"Look there," she said. "They got Save-Marts all the way up here now."

"Yeah, they're everywhere now. It's all made in China, so what the hell, huh?"

"I got nothing against Chinese," Jane said.

"I know I like eggrolls," Cheryle said.

"Can we stop there?"

"We can," Cheryle said.

As they were walking into the store, just as they were past the electronic doors, a lady let out a squeal and ran over to Cheryle. She was a short lady with an ass that made it look as if she was pulling a trailer. She had two little boys with her.

"Oh, my god. Are you Cheryle Banker?"

Cheryle smiled. "Today. Yesterday. And tomorrow."

"You're my favorite. That song about the pasture and the grass and such. I love that."

"Hay."

"What?" said the woman.

"Pasture and hay. But it doesn't matter. Glad you like it."

"Oh, we all like it. We got all your albums. And that cover of Johnny Cash's "Home of the Blues" is so good. Me and the boys, we put that on and dance around the house to your songs."

"I'm flattered," Cheryle said.

"Would you sign a piece a paper for us. I don't have one of your CDs with me, but I'm so excited to meet you."

"Of course. Because you recognized me, I'd sign a paper bag you wanted."

The lady began to scuttle about in her purse for paper and pen.

Cheryle said, "I'm going to visit here a moment. Why don't you and Henry shop around and I'll catch up?"

Jane and Henry nodded and walked off, leaving Cheryle chatting away with the woman and her two sons. That smile of Cheryle and the way she looked and the excitement of the lady talking to her was causing others to come over and investigate.

"I don't think she'll quit music at all," Henry said. "See her light up?"

"Like a fire cracker. I wish I had something I could do that I was good at and I liked doing it."

"Don't we all."

Jane and Henry went to the section with kitchen appliances, and there Jane saw it. One was on display on top of a cardboard box. It sparkled in the store light like a vein of silver. It was the Super Toaster. It was long and it had a clock on it that was so well defined you could see it from a goodly distance and make out the time. It wasn't digital time. It was an old-fashioned clock with a face and hands, and besides its shiny silver, there were black and red knobs on it. There were little cartoon characters painted on the ends of it, though Jane couldn't figure out what kind of characters they were. Gnomes with hats maybe, though maybe they were elves. It was an odd thing to have on the toaster, but it damn sure livened it up.

As they came to it, Henry said, "Damn. That looks like the kind of toaster they'd use on the space shuttle, some little village on Mars."

Jane read on the box under it. It kept time. It toasted all at once, or one at a time. It sprayed butter on the toast if you wanted to do that, and it could brown one, darken another, and leave one lightly toasted, and whatever you wanted with another. Or they could all go dark, or light, or anywhere in between. It was all there at the touch of a knob or two.

"Mars, hell. This is Pluto stuff," Jane said.

"That isn't a planet anymore."

Jane checked the price. "It's expensive."

"We're talking quality, Jane. That's the kind of item that might outlive us all. It's the goddamn motherlode of toasters."

Jane took one of the unopened boxes and tucked it under her arm. "Let's check out."

TWENTY-ONE

WHEN they arrived in Boston at the bus station, Cheryle pulled over to the curb, said, "I feel like a toad for not taking you where you need to go, Jane, but to tell you true I'm tight on my schedule. I got some gigs here in Boston, and a couple of the places even have toilets where the floor doesn't stick to your shoes."

"Now that's class," Henry said.

"Darn tootin'."

"I'm just glad you can drop Henry off where she needs to go," Jane said.

"Where do you need to go, Henry?" Cheryle asked.

Henry rattled off the address and the doctor's name. "My appointment is tomorrow morning at ten. I have an evaluation of some sort. All kind of iffy, really. I'm going to stay at some motel close to the office, if I can find one."

"I'll look it up on my phone, find a close motel," Cheryle said. "Hey, they can't fix your eye, let me tell you, you fucking rock that patch."

"Thanks, Cheryle. I'm going to walk Jane into the station."

"Good luck, girl, and look, here's my card. Give me a call sometime. You're bored, maybe we can rob a filling station or beat up some kids for lunch money."

"Sounds like a plan," Jane said as she took the card. She tucked the bagged toaster under her arm, and with her purse slung over her shoulder, got out of the convertible, followed by Henry, who was carrying Jane's suitcase, the panty bag now stuck inside of it. Throwing the old cow doodie stained pants and shirt away had given the suitcase more room.

Jane looked back at Cheryle. "Been a pleasure spending time with you."

Cheryle smiled. "Hell, I know that."

Jane and Henry walked into the station. Jane examined the bus schedule posted on a screen. A lot of people were going to a lot of places. She hated buses, but it was a short trip, so she decided she had to buck up.

"That toaster might cause you back trouble by the time you get there," Henry said.

"It is heavy... So, I guess this is goodbye."

"Yep. It's been all right."

"Now, don't go all out, Henry."

"Okay. It wasn't that much fun."

Jane smiled. "Some of it was."

"My favorite part was seeing that fat ass bitch drown."

"I don't know how I feel about that," Jane said, "but I will say I don't miss the mosquito."

"We might see each other back home," Henry said.

"Yeah. We might. Well, I got to go. I still got to get my ticket."

Henry nodded. Jane used her free hand to pat Henry on the shoulder. Henry reached out and hugged her. Jane hugged her back.

"That's my one hug for the year," Henry said. "Maybe three or four years. You take care."

"I will. You too."

"Hell, I can bench press two-hundred pounds and shit a rose bush with the thorns on it. I'll be all right."

Henry left Jane's luggage, turned and walked away, through the glass doors. Jane could see Cheryle waiting at the curb, raising a hand to wave. Jane waved back, and taking hold of her luggage, went to get her ticket.

THE bus wasn't as bad as she remembered, but maybe it was because the trip was so short. When she got off the bus with her goods, she was surprised at how warm it was. She always thought of the north as cold, even though it was still summer. She looked at the address she had written down. She walked over to a filling station pulling her luggage, the toaster under her arm, and asked where the motel was, just to be certain.

"You're right on top of it," said a man in greasy work clothes. His accent threw Jane a little, but she got it figured. He walked her out of the station and pointed to a sign that had the motel's name on it.

"Oh, had it been a snake it would have bitten me."

"It's a motel."

"Yes. Right."

Jane walked pulling her luggage after her, still hugging the toaster under her arm. She was sweaty when she arrived at the motel. She asked an attractive Asian lady behind the desk where the wedding was to be, found out it was to be in the main ball room, "Or as main as a motel ballroom gets," the lady said in a Yankee accent Jane only understood through careful listening.

Jane nodded, and then asked if there was a room available. She held her breath, not having reserved a room in advance.

There was a room on the first floor. The swimming pool was right outside the sliding doors, the lady at the desk said.

Jane used her credit card, which she had carefully avoided until now. She got her key and went to her room. She checked the time. The wedding was three hours away, and right down the hall. She opened the curtains and looked at the pool. A fat boy with a white swan float wrapped around him jumped in the water and splashed a woman in a pool chair who was most likely his mother. The woman yelled at him. Jane pulled the curtains.

There was a coffee maker in the room, and Jane made coffee, but didn't drink much of it because it tasted like a rat had shit in the cup. She stalled for another hour watching TV. It was mostly stuff she didn't want to see, and the stuff she did want to see she wouldn't have time to finish, so she turned it off. She could hear the boy and more kids now yelling in the pool outside. She heard the mother yell, "Better settle down, you little shits."

Jane took her time taking a shower. She wore a plastic shower cap she had brought to keep from dampening her hair, which she had washed the night before.

She got out of the shower and looked at herself in the mirror. Alright, no one was going to put her on the cover of *Vogue,* but she looked alright. She dried off and removed the shower cap and shook out her hair and posed in front of the long mirror in the bedroom a few times for no good reason other than she felt like it. She put on her makeup and pulled on the dress Cheryle had given her. It fit her like a paint job. She moved around in it a bit and decided she was satisfied. If she danced some, nothing was going to rip.

Okay. I'm here, she said to herself. That's what counts.

She took a deep breath and sat on the bed and put on socks and pulled on the bright blue boots with the yellow stars, and pushed the bills from her other shoe down into the sock inside her right boot. She looked in the mirror again.

She damn sure looked taller, and that was a plus, though she thought she looked dressed for a square dance or a late date with Smokey Bear, who she assumed was a country music fan for some reason. Maybe she needed a hat like his to set her wardrobe off.

She was nervous. She hadn't seen her sisters in years, and the younger one was the one she most didn't want to see, and it was her wedding. But she had defied the odds, and was going to surprise those blood-kin bitches by showing up. She was going to dance to the music and eat too much and maybe get drunk and fall over something and maybe piss herself during the toasts.

That euphoric feeling didn't maintain. Right then, the idea of arriving at the wedding by means of spite didn't have quite the satisfying emotional bite it had when she was at home in Texas. She felt displaced and strange and remarkably anxious. After being on the road, the adventures she had with Henry, everything felt a little lightweight. She thought she should really feel bad about General Mumu and her minions, but realized she truly didn't; just believed she should.

Maybe that wasn't a good sign. Maybe she was a bad person. And maybe as Henry had said, it was the others who were bad and to hell with them.

Jane found her invitation to the wedding and took hold of it with all the desperation of a drowning woman clutching a straw.

She stood before the mirror one more time, said, "Fuck it. I look good."

There was no way she was going to be able to wrap the toaster and make it look presentable, so she decided to keep it in the bag. She took hold of the bag and went out into the hallway and began to march toward the room where the wedding was to be held. Maybe her outfit would look more correct at the steak house reception.

As she neared the room where the wedding was to be held, she saw a table in the hall, near the wall, and behind it she saw one of her sisters sitting there. She was wearing a very nice blue dress and she leaned forward and looked down the length of the table as Jane approached. She stood up and walked away, and before Jane could reach the check in table, her other sisters came forward, the younger one wearing a wedding dress that looked to have cost enough to burn out a credit card or two. The others wore blue and looked so much alike they might have been matching barbie dolls. They all had blonde hair and long legs and looked as if they had been polished with a damp rag. They had enough Botox in their faces to cause them to look in a state of perpetual surprise.

The oldest one, May, said, "Damn girl. You made it."

Jane placed her invitation on the table. "Yeah. It was quite a haul."

"We never got a confirmation," the next to youngest, Carolyn said. "We didn't expect you to be here."

"I know. Sorry. Wasn't sure I'd make it. Had some car trouble. But I'm here."

"Yes," Ronnie said. "You are."

"You going to get dressed," Jennifer said.

"I am dressed," Jane said.

Ronnie, the bride-to-be, studied Jane, said, "For what? Barrel racing?"

"I consider this all purpose."

"I don't know, Jane," Ronnie said. "I mean, you came all the way, and I appreciate that, but there's a certain decorum expected for something like this."

Jane stood there holding her sack with the toaster.

"Decorum?"

"Yes. It's a wedding. Are those rhinestones?"

"Talk about decorum, you're wearing white like you're a virgin. Hell, that child you got arrive by immaculate conception?"

"It's traditional," Ronnie said. "You can't just show up looking like you been standing on a street corner at the intersection of Hee-haw and Gooberville and expect to come in and join us. Everyone is wearing blue, except me, of course. You don't wear red and rhinestones to a wedding."

"I'm just here for the wedding. I'm not a bridesmaid. I wasn't asked."

"It was just so far for you to come," May said.

"Listen," Ronnie said. "No offense, but Jane, the rest of us have brought a certain sophistication to the family, and you're still cussing and talking and dressing like a slut. That dress was an inch shorter, you'd have to powder another set of cheeks."

"Damn," Jane said. "Really? I remember when you ate boogers, Ronnie. I remember when you used to shit outside behind the carport, right beside a big ole clay dirt daubers nest. You'd just squat, lean against the wall and let it fly."

"I did not," Ronnie said.

"Actually, you did," May said.

"I was a baby."

"Seven years old, I think," May said, but then she realized she was wading into uncharted waters and cleared her throat.

"And the high school football team called you pin cushion," Jane said. "And it wasn't because you were sewing up their uniforms."

"That was a misunderstanding," Ronnie said.

"It was about two hours in the back seat of a car parked on Humper's Hill was what it was."

"You ought not to say things like that," Ronnie said.

Jane took a moment to consider. Her eyes roamed over her sisters like she was seeing them for the first time.

"And the rest of you, you're nothing special either. You're just country people like me, only you live in the north, and it's cold up here, or will be soon, so I tell you what, ladies, I realized just this minute, I don't have a damn thing in common with any of you. Maybe you have become sophisticated or some such. I don't know. But I met a one-eyed, muscle-lady and a struggling country singer, and I knew both of them a lot less time than I've known all of you, and you know what? I like them better. A lot better. They're who they are and that's all they are, and they're interesting. You wouldn't be interesting, none of you, if you had propellers up your asses and you could fly around the room with them."

"We're your sisters," Jennifer said. "That's not nice."

"But it's true. I have always felt like a swan among assholes, if you want to know the truth, and now I'm certain of it. You know, I came thinking I ought to be here out of spite, and then I realized I might really want to see all of you, and now I realize I don't. But don't say I'm a sore loser. Me and my barrel racing dress are going to go, but here's your goddamn wedding present. It's a doozy. A Super Toaster, and let me tell you, this shiny little shit will not only toast bread, it will toast up to four slices in any order and degree you want, and while you're waiting, you can check the goddamn time, and you can butter the bread while it's toasting, and when it's done, what I suggest, is you each take a slice of that well-prepared toast and shove a piece up each of your asses, and Ronnie, you can then shove the toaster up your butt without the butter to lubricate it. And let me pass along my congratulations on your wedding day in a cheap-ass motel, you self-righteous bitch."

Jane placed the sack with the toaster on the reception table. Jane turned and wagged her ass in a big way as she walked off.

"Well, I never," Jennifer said.

"I don't doubt that," Jane said without looking back, and made her way back to her room.

When she got there, she sat on the bed and looked around. She looked in the mirror. She began to cry, and then went to the bathroom and dampened a towel and placed it across her face as she lay on the bed and heaved in anger.

"Bitches," she said.

Eventually she removed the towel, sat up and used the motel phone to call the bus station.

Finished, she got up and put her suitcase back together. She took a deep breath, sobbed once, then quit.

As she left her room she looked down the hall. May was back behind the table, and the other sisters were still clustered around. They looked at her. Jane shot them the finger and pulled her luggage out of the hotel and made her way to the bus station.

She sat on a bench for up to an hour after buying her ticket. After a bit she got up and put some coins in a machine and got some peanut butter crackers, and then from another machine a Diet Coke. She sat back down and ate the crackers and drank the soda.

When it was time, and she was finally on board and the bus was moving, she glanced at the motel where the wedding was happening and felt a pang of regret, but nothing like she expected. It only hurt a little, like pulling a thorn out of your toes.

The route back to Boston made more stops than the trip from Boston, so it was nightfall when she arrived at the bus station. She hadn't felt bothered by the bus trip at all. She found a hotel next to the bus station and used her credit card there, and was happy again that she was not declined.

The room was shabby and she was famished. She asked for a seven-thirty wake up call, pulled off her boots, then laid down on the bed wearing the dress Cheryle had given her, living with her hunger.

She awoke to the phone ringing. Her wake up call.

She sat up and remembered the address Henry had given for her doctor. She wrote it down on a piece of motel stationary with an inconsistent ink pen. She stripped off the dress and showered with her plastic shower cap on, put the dress and boots back on, gathered up the things she had removed from the suitcase, loaded it, and pulled it out into the lobby. They had a free breakfast in the motel, so she had a waffle with syrup and two sausage patties that tasted like drink coasters. She had two cups of coffee and a carton of milk and a blackened banana.

There was a taxi out front of the motel. She got in, gave him the paper she had written Henry's doctor's address on, said, "Can you take me there?"

"Of course," the driver said. He looked to be in his thirties. He wore a pork pie hat with the front of the brim pushed up and he had a blond chin beard. He looked like a jazz musician. He was not bad looking. He glanced over the seat at her.

"How far is it?" Jane asked.

"It's not close, but traffic isn't so bad."

"Good. I'd like to be there by nine, if possible."

"Maybe we can do that, pretty close anyway. I like that dress."

"Thank you. So do I."

"I say if you got it, flaunt it. I didn't mean that sexist, by the way."

"Not at all. You couldn't have said anything better."

"You sound Southern."

"East Texas."

"I love that accent."

"Why thank you."

They pulled away and Jane watched as the traffic moved by and they passed Yankee buildings. They were all so unique. She had never been to any big cities outside of Texas, and Boston had a different air about it. Or maybe it just seemed that way.

When they arrived at the address, Jane fished some bills from inside her sock and paid the driver and tipped him and got out with her suitcase. It was a brown building with a long row of steps that led to a cement landing and glass doors.

"This is it?" she said through the driver's open window.

"It is. I think you need to go up the stairs. That should be the address, in the building."

"All right."

"Wait a moment." The driver got out of the taxi and took hold of her suitcase. "Let's make sure. I'm okay here for a moment."

He pushed the extended handle in and carried the luggage up to the landing and pointed at numbers above the glass door.

"There you are. You can see the name and numbers better from here."

"Thanks," Jane said.

The driver took a card from inside his coat and held it out to her. "Get bored, here's my number. Just to show you around, maybe buy you dinner. I got the feeling you haven't been here before."

"That's right. I'll take the card and think about it."

"All I ask."

The driver shook her hand and walked down the steps. He looked back up at her. He really was handsome, but he could lose that beard, Jane thought. It belonged on a goat.

He drove the taxi away and Jane pulled her suitcase through the glass doors.

INSIDE she looked at the doctor's name on the plaque on the wall, then she saw what it said out beside it. She went through another set of glass doors and spoke to a woman at a desk in the lobby, and the woman went away and came back with Henry.

"I'm surprised to see you," Henry said.

"The wedding didn't interest me as much as I had hoped."

"Won't they miss you?"

"Naw. They'll figure I went to shit and the hogs ate me."

"Well, you found me."

"You gave me the doctor's name. I knew the time of your appointment."

Henry nodded. "I guess you know this isn't an eye doctor?"

"I just found out. Read it on the plaque."

"How do you feel about that?"

"Like I want to wait with you."

Henry nodded, went back through another glass door and Jane followed, pulling her luggage. They stopped at a long desk surrounded by glass with a smiling short-haired blond man seated behind it.

"This is my friend. Can she wait with me?"

"I don't see why not," he said. He had nice teeth.

"His name is Reggie."

"Hi, Reggie. I'm Jane."

"Glad to make your acquaintance," Reggie said.

They sat in two chairs at one end of a row of chairs about six feet from the desk. There were magazines on a table next to Jane and a TV screen was hung above the desk on metal supports that stuck out beyond the glass covering and the TV sound was turned off. It was on a nature channel. Instinctively, Jane looked up at it.

"I don't know why they have it on," Henry said. "With the sound off."

"Yeah. That seems like a silly idea. Are you okay?"

"I don't know."

"I can assume this will not change your eye one bit."

"Correct. But it will change something else."

"You been planning this for a while, I guess."

"I did without a lot of things to save for it. I have a place here, Jane. I'm paid up for a year. I check into the place tonight. It wasn't ready for me until today. I'm getting a consultation today, then I'm going to have some tests, and then I'm going to start taking certain shots and then, later, I'll begin the transition. Are you surprised?"

"A little."

"Does it matter?"

"Nope. I mean, it might take some getting used to."

"I been feeling like I was someone else for a long time, since I was a kid, and now I want to be that other person that I think is really me."

"You'll be able to pee standing up."

"You know. I haven't thought about that little plus. They have connections for all of it here. The surgeries, I mean. It's not like an in and out operation. You got hormone doctors, plastic surgeons, and so on. It's not all the one doctor. I even got insurance covers some of it. Today is just the first day. Nothing big happens today."

"I suppose that depends on how you look at it."

"Yeah. I guess so. You know, Jane. You're my only friend."

"Think I'd be here if I had another friend?"

Henry laughed.

Jane nudged Henry slightly with her elbow. "How big is the apartment?"

"Big enough for a guest."

"For a few days?"

"Yeah. I mean, you'd have to sleep on the couch. My place. My bed."

"You ought to sleep in another room."

"Why?"

"I don't want to hear you snore."

"I don't snore that bad."

"Oh yes you do."

"There won't be any mosquitoes."

"That's good. Hey. I met a taxi driver that wants to show me around town. He was cute."

"He'd know his way around, wouldn't he?"

"I bet he would." Jane glanced at the TV. "Those little meerkats are cute, aren't they?"

"They make me think of weasels."

They were quiet for a time, watching the silent TV. A meerkat had popped up out of a hole in the ground and was looking anxiously about. Henry was looking at that when she said, "You know. I been wanting this for a long time, and now I'm a little scared. Maybe a lot scared."

"I'm here with you," Jane said, and took Henry's hand and squeezed it.

They sat that way for a while, holding hands, and finally a young woman in a light blue nurse outfit came through a door and called Henry's name.